A BOWDON Romance

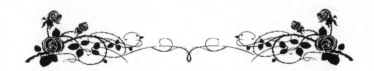

Alice Frank

Alice Frank

A
BOWDON
Romance

MEMOIRS

Cirencester

Published by Memoirs

MEMOIRS
PUBLISHING

Memoirs Books

25 Market Place, Cirencester, Gloucestershire, GL7 2NX
info@memoirsbooks.co.uk   www.memoirspublishing.com

First published in England, April 2012

Cover montage:
Village scene - Copyright The Francis Frith Collection®
Couple - victorianpicturelibrary.com

ISBN 978-1-909020-07-8

Printed in England

Also by Alice Frank - A Dangerous Obsession
The true-life ordeal of two women who were driven almost to the point of madness by an obsessive stalker
and a misguided social worker who backed him up - by trying to get one of them certified

A BOWDON Romance

Contents

A Bowdon Romance

Stories from history

ACKNOWLEDGMENTS

I should like to thank David Miller for his help in advising me on historical aspects of this story. Other material was kindly supplied by Steve Cliffe, Editor, *Stockport and District Heritage*. Some material has been drawn from *Classic Murders of the North-East*, by Albert A Thompson.

Chapter One

DOWN MEMORY LANE

It was 1850, and Charlotte had just got off the train at Bowdon Station at the bottom of the Downs. It was only one short stop from Altrincham Station at that time along the Stockport Road. When she had first heard about the new trains, she had always said she'd never go in one. They were dangerous. She knew that when Queen Victoria had first travelled by train the newspapers had said that although they very much admired her courage, they hoped she would never take such a risk again.

Now Charlotte had taken the same risk. She had travelled from Stockport to Altrincham, then on one more stop to Bowdon Station, but she vowed she would never do it again. She especially felt that she should not have put her eight-year-old daughter Tooty at such risk by taking her with her.

'We'll keep to the passenger boat on the canal next time' she told her, but Tooty hoped they wouldn't. She loved going fast.

Bowdon Station was at the corner of Railway Street and Hale Moss on Pinfold Brow, later to be called Lloyd Street. How different it looked to her from Stockport, that dirty, overcrowded place everyone had flocked to in order to work in the mills. She stood outside the railway station facing it. How glorious the Downs was, almost all agricultural land, with its fertile cultivated gardens, winding, narrow lanes with thick hedges on both sides and leafy trees hanging over them, with cottages dotted here and there.

It was not surprising that she found it all so breathtaking, for all had been peaceful for such a long time. Even going back as far as the Civil War of 1644, the only disturbance had been when Prince Rupert had stopped for a short time with his army of men on the way to win Chester back again for the Royalists. It had been besieged by Sir William Brereton, a prominent Parliamentarian leader. Prince Rupert soon marched on to Cheadle, where the enemy immediately ran away.

Four years later a meeting of Lieutenancy was held in Bowdon and plans were made to recruit many more men, but without success. The locals didn't want to enrol under the banner of the King, which may have been due to the local influence of George Booth, an active supporter of the Parliamentarians.

41 years later, in 1685, there was another disturbance on Bowdon Downs when a Robert Radcliffe, aged 30, was killed in a duel in a field later to be called Radcliffe's Croft. It saddened a lot of people, and was something they couldn't understand. Why had those two men quarrelled, and was it just unlucky that they happened to meet the next day? Yet apart from these two things, life on Bowdon Downs had run smoothly along.

Charlotte was struck by the beauty of the pear tree in the garden of the house on the corner of Thorley Moor, later to be called Ashley Road. She thought how beautiful it must look at blossom time. In fact everything around her was magnificent. Railway Street had only just been given a name - it had been regarded before as part of the Downs with its meadows, market gardens and the few cottages it had.

She looked to the other side of her at Hale Moss, Lloyd Street. Here she saw several small cottages, a village blacksmith, a timber yard and a butcher's shop. She shuddered, hating the thought of killing animals. She never ate meat.

The Warburtons ran the horse slaughterers at Hale Moss and for two or three generations members of the family were called 'Salty' Warburton because of the large quantities of salt they used and got covered in. One person later used to say that the last he remembered of them was a woman who used to drive a horse and cart wearing a leather apron and cap and smoking a pipe, still called 'Salty' (going back to Victorian times, they were probably always called 'Salty').

Charlotte didn't look to see how much further Hale Moss went, as it stretched along into land which was mainly just brambles and gorse, called Goose Green. She knew it was only a five-minute walk to the home of Betsy Warburton, a woman now elderly who hadn't been well. She lived in a small terraced house in a square of such houses, also called Goose Green. Charlotte knew she should go and see her, but she couldn't go just then.

Betsy lived there with her son-in-law and grandson and granddaughter, and they were all on parish relief. Goose Green hadn't always been peaceful - indeed at times it had been bedlam with disputes, especially in the last two years. The people resented it very much that Lord Stamford was selling parts of it to builders. They wanted it for common land, as they could use it for several purposes. The people of Altrincham had the use of it to graze cattle, horses, donkeys, geese and ducks.

Tooty held Charlotte's hand as she crossed the road and started to walk towards Bowdon. She had been told the way. 'Follow the paths on the Bowdon Downs until you come to Burying Lane, facing Bowdon Church, then you'll soon find Richmond Road' she had been told. She didn't want to go that way. It wasn't only that it looked so formidable, all those winding paths, with the bushes and trees; it was also the name, Burying Lane. She knew why it was called this. It was where a funeral procession would go along on its way to Bowdon Church. She hated this thought as she had suffered so much bereavement herself.

Burying Lane had been fully described to her. 'You'll soon recognize it,' someone had tried to assure her. It was no more than a sandy lane lying deep among a clump of fir trees with bushes on either side. She wondered why they didn't call it The Firs instead. She didn't know that one day they would.

She started on her way, walking up and up the Downs and always following the same path. Someone had told her there was a house half way up called Half Way House because it was a place where people could stop and rest. She couldn't see it. Soon she saw two cottages and another somewhat bigger house, which although still on the Downs had been slightly separated from the rest of it. It had been named Wellington Place following the victory of the Duke of Wellington.

She walked on, to find that she was going in completely the wrong direction; in fact she was heading towards a slum, so she decided to go back to the station and start again. She made up her mind not to go that way at all.

From Bowdon Station she started along Thorley Moor, passing a big pear tree and some small cottages on the left hand side. They had been built at the end of the seventeenth century.

'Straight on, straight on' her friend Gloria had told her, if she decided to take that path. She wondered why they didn't call it Ashley Road, as it was on the way to Ashley; it made things so much easier if things had a descriptive name. She didn't know that one day it would indeed be called Ashley Road.

Then she came to a narrow lane called St John's Road. So far it had all been just gardens, fields, farm buildings, stables, all a part of the Downs. There wasn't much more down St John's Road - it was mainly stables.

She walked on. She wasn't certain where one road or lane changed into another, and she began to panic. Now Thorley Moor was taking a big curve to the left on its way to Ashley, so she turned into it. She found herself in a place criss-crossed by streams, called Peel Causeway.

She hadn't gone far when she saw an old farmhouse, so she knew she was going the wrong way. Someone had told her it was where they intended building another station, which in 1902 would become Hale Station. The station master would live in the farmhouse. Someone else said a vet was going to buy it and start up a practice there, but they said that wouldn't be for a long, long time.

'I'm going the wrong way' she thought, and again she turned back. She found herself sometimes jumping across streams and heading towards a mill. Then, as she walked along a small patch of waste land, she turned left before going past the mill. There was also a cottage there, a field called Butty Croft and an orchard called Well Croft.

She found herself approaching another lane, later to be called Langham Road, with some very big houses on both sides. She now felt certain she was on her way to Bowdon.

Next she saw a hut. Gloria had told her to turn right when she came to a hut and said that as she walked up a hill she would find herself on the corner of Richmond Road and East Downs Road. She did turn right, but soon realised she was going up no hill. There was a pond here and men were fishing. How she wished they wouldn't kill animals, she hated it. Just when she was about to turn back one of the fishermen called across to her.

'Are you lost?'

'Yes, is this Heald Common, where they're going to build Heald Road?' she asked.

'Well it is Heald Common, I do know that. No doubt one day they'll build a road here called that' he told her. 'Where do you want to go?'

'I'm looking for some new houses in Richmond Road.'

He looked pleased that he could help her. 'Go to Sandy Lane' he said, pointing at the road straight ahead. 'Turn left and go to the top and you'll find Richmond Road.'

She was so relieved, and she set off as instructed. On the way she started talking to a man who was also walking up it, who said he'd take her all the way.

'I'm so glad they call it Sandy Lane, something descriptive' she told him, for indeed it was a sandy one. He agreed. Then he spoiled it all by saying, 'I'm afraid they are going to change the name. They are going to call it Stamford Road, after Lord Stamford.'

'Well I wish they wouldn't' she told him. To hell with Lord Stamford, she thought.

When she reached the top she knew where she was. It was all as her friend Gloria had told her. There was a square called the Polygon with a horse-drawn bus service for passengers. She saw the Griffin public house and Bowdon Church across the square from it. She had vaguely heard something about bear-baiting and bull-baiting just outside the church gate. They would tie the animal up and get dogs to attack it.

She shuddered - she hoped it was not true. But she had nothing to worry about. It had all been stopped a long time ago, in 1820, by the Reverend Law, of Bowdon Church. He had greatly influenced public opinion by expressing his disapproval.

She turned down the hill and found herself in Richmond Road. She was nearly there. She reached the end of it, the part Gloria had told her about, where it curved round into East Downs Road. She looked straight ahead of her and found herself facing a wilderness. She thought that amid the shrubbery she could see a well, and then she clearly saw a goat, and then another.

How she wished people wouldn't keep goats, for they drank such a lot of water and people needed the water a lot more than they needed the milk. She knew something about it - that a goat or cow with milk will drink as much as 15 pints of water a day. And if only all that land to grow food for them could be used to grow something like potatoes for people, or just left for trees. The leaves would make good compost for growing more vegetables. In fact there were so many ways of getting the garden to grow without manure.

She had been told that they intended building more big houses there. They wanted to extend Richmond Road so that it went right down to the bottom to meet Langham Road, and then East Downs Road would only be a road off it. She did hope so. More jobs for her away from the slums.

She walked along East Downs Road until she came to the house she wanted. It was where Gloria worked as a servant girl, and where she hoped both she and Tooty would be able to get a job. She knew it had some good cellars and that Gloria had made them practically her home. She understood that these cellars had good windows which kept out the cold but let in light. Maybe she could live in those cellars, with no muck coming in through the walls as they did in some slums, including the ones in Altrincham. Although her main ambition had been to avoid ever having to live in such overcrowded conditions, she did not want to get out of it by being a servant girl in some of the houses she had heard about. She knew that sometimes they would have to sleep in the kitchen or in cupboards under the stairs. They were forbidden to sing or laugh, and had to be as silent and as invisible as possible. Gloria told her that although she kept as separate as she could from the Carltons, it was nothing like as bad as that.

Charlotte's husband had been dead for some years. She was determined not to have to go back to the Union Workhouse in Shaw Heath, Stockport. She knew it all too well - men breaking stones until they fitted through fine mesh, she never knew what for. Women picking oakum - something to do with string filling in portholes on boats - and that was all she did know. Those who were ill, but still able to crawl, were left to scrub the floors. Charlotte had worked in the laundry, but soon left. She would rather sleep rough than have either her child or herself bullied. It wasn't only the staff; it would sometimes be the other inmates.

What had finally made her snap was someone offering to teach Tooty to ride a horse. It was an old friend of hers, Jacob, who had worked with her husband in some stables. The workhouse were grumbling about it and not letting her go. Charlotte walked out.

Jacob worked for some rich people who were away a lot, and sometimes Charlotte had been able to make the stables her home. At other times she and Tooty had had to sleep in shop doorways, though not for long. She had managed to get a job. It wasn't in a big house. It only had two floors and four bedrooms upstairs, and although it wasn't badly furnished there was nothing luxurious about it. It was far from the conventional upstairs, downstairs grand home.

She and Tooty shared a biggish room on the ground floor which should really have been the dining room. It looked out on to the back, a biggish garden that Charlotte loved. It had a tank for collecting rain water and as long as they didn't use too much there was always enough for them. There was also a standpipe in the road shared between many households. The toilet, called the privy, was kept outside.

Charlotte was pleased about it all, for she felt certain that polluted water was causing such diseases as cholera, typhus and dysentery. Many health officials thought this, but others weren't so sure. They said maybe it was simply something in the air. That made sense – the air certainly stank.

Still, big attempts were being made to get more pipes laid down. Plenty of people felt it was important not to mix water from the sewer with the drinking water. In Altrincham in the 1850s they did start to put some very big pipes under the ground, with a plan that maybe one day they'd be able to connect them to the houses so that every household could have clean running water. The most important part was to keep them away from sewers. What a risk to take, to spend all that money, if at the end of it all it was discovered that the disease was nothing to do with the water!

But for now everything seemed to be going well where Charlotte was prepared to settle. She loved the garden. It was a wilderness; A hedgehog had his home there and wild flowers were growing everywhere. Only flowers - the people she worked for bought their vegetables from a neighbour. Many a night, after a day's work, Charlotte would sit at the window looking out. Sometimes she would go and pick the flowers and put them into a vase in the hall, or in the window in the front room for anyone to see going past.

It was a middle-aged couple in Bramhall who employed her, a Mr and Mrs Martin. They had a business together, went out to some office every day and left Charlotte to do everything. It was not much more than cleaning and cooking. Although she got all the food for herself and Tooty, they paid her next to nothing. However, she could do what she liked in her own time, pop out to the stables with Tooty, or spend some time hearing her read.

How glorious it would have been if those times had continued, but after a while she began to realise something funny was going on. Then she found out what it was - the Martins were both drinking. Drink was nothing short of poison to Charlotte. There'd be no knowing what might happen next.

The first incident was when she came in and found that Mrs Martin had been trying to hang some washing on the line outside. This was in the back garden. It was news to Charlotte that she ever did any - anything like that was usually left to her. Mrs Martin had fallen into a heap on the ground. Charlotte was horrified when she saw it, and for a moment she thought she was dead. She hardly dared go out to have a close look. When she did, Mrs Martin stirred and said, 'I've only had two half glasses of wine.' The woman next door leaned over the fence and said, 'I think you forget the full ones you have in between.'

Charlotte started trying to get her up, but she refused to co-operate and seemed to want to lie there. The woman next door said 'Leave her' - she was clearly used to it. Charlotte went back inside, deciding that everything would sort itself out just as long as it didn't pour with rain.

Things were back to normal the next day and remained so for a while after. Then one day they had a dinner party. Although only four people came, it meant Charlotte had a lot to do. They told her to have an early night and to leave the clearing up until next morning, and she went to bed.

At one in the morning she was woken by Mrs Martin outside her door shouting, 'I'm very annoyed. I'm very annoyed!'. It startled Charlotte. The first thing that came to mind was that it was about the washing up and she had forgotten that she had told her to leave it. But it wasn't that - it was the guests she was shouting at. They were right outside Charlotte's door, and were saying quietly to one another, 'What's she annoyed about?'

Charlotte wondered if they realised she was drunk. She was very glad that Tooty was sleeping through it all. Then the guests all crept quietly away, and like the incident in the garden it soon blew over.

It was when the nephew Eddie came round that she really felt she had had enough. Mrs Martin was shouting at him, and he shouted straight back at her, loud and clear, 'Aunty, you're drunk!'

Tooty was frightened. Eddie stopped it when he saw that, but he later told Charlotte that Mr and Mrs Martin were well known around certain pubs for rowing and brawling. Charlotte witnessed these drunken brawls often, and once when she pushed a chest of drawers up against the door to stop Mrs Martin getting in, she was awoken in the middle of the night by her pushing on it.

'What do you want?' she called out to her.

'Can you lend me half a crown?'

'No!'

She went away, but whatever was she thinking of? She knew Charlotte was completely dependent on her for money. She couldn't stand it any more, so she left. It was back to sleeping in shop doorways and then back to the workhouse.

It may have surprised people that she got away with leaving like this. Walking out was not as easy as it sounds. It was more like the next time she went to church she just didn't go back again. There could be punishments for going, yet Charlotte got away with it.

She discovered that the Matron did have some sort of conscience. 'Don't go again, or at least not until Tooty has fully mastered reading and writing, she mustn't lose any more lessons' she told her, smiling. She had found out that she couldn't always use force.

'Oh yes,' thought Charlotte, 'And she may never have had another chance to learn to ride a horse.' She had spent so much of her young days mucking out stables that she had learned to ride, and now she had made certain that Tooty could.

Workhouses were first set up with good intentions, and sometimes with good results. One man involved in starting them died a happy man. He said, 'Now plenty of old people are living in comfort.' And there were other good results from them; girls were given a trade, in spinning. Then everything went horribly wrong.

Although they went on giving relief to the poor, which was called 'indoor relief' they became increasingly squalid and overcrowded. Yet still families stayed together.

Sometimes it was made possible for people to live in their own homes and they were given a bit of money, and this was called 'outdoor relief'. Then it started getting abused. People were going for help who didn't need it. These scroungers wrecked it for everyone. It made people afraid to give. Sometimes they felt very silly if they'd given to someone who turned out not to be needy.

Everything changed when they passed the Poor Act in 1834. Now very few people could get outdoor relief. Mostly the needy could get nothing unless they went into the workhouse. Families were split up, husband and wife couldn't even sleep in the same dormitories and they exercised in different yards. Babies usually stayed with their mothers until they were old enough to go for lessons, but even this wasn't always kept. The reason given was that if they weren't very hard on them, people would accept their support who didn't need it. But solving the problem this way created another. It attracted power freaks. They were applying for jobs there, and their interest wasn't to help the poor, it was to enjoy making them accept what they didn't want to accept.

When Charlotte had first gone in, she had been interviewed by the board, and then issued with a uniform. It was all right, she liked it, a long white apron and a plain dress with it, but some of the women couldn't stand it. It made them feel they had been sent to prison.

She had been in the workhouse during the big riot of 1842, the General Strike. It had been more like civil war. The noise had been just dreadful. First they were trying to break down the outside gate. 'Oh no!' she cried out, and the others around her were panicking and hoping they wouldn't succeed, but they did. Then they proceeded to break down the inner door. She could hear them crashing away and wondered if they would kill her. She clung so hard to Tooty.

Then the worst happened. The rioters were all inside. They were everywhere. She hid in a corner, still clinging to Tooty.

Still hanging on to Tooty, she rushed out of the door and down to St Thomas's church. The door was wide open. The vicar, the

Reverend Henry Bellair, had dared to open it for a short while, feeling it would be safe as long as he was right by the door and ready to lock it should there be any sign of the rioters getting close. He had two other people with him. He wanted to be there to make certain that anyone in distress, like Charlotte, could get in. There had been chaos all day, people rushing everywhere with the latest news, police arriving from Dunham Massey, Manchester and Altrincham. The place was also swarming with soldiers.

Charlotte missed the Reverend Martin Gilpin, who had died at 37. He had been her rock. He had been 23 when he had first taken the post at St Thomas's, which had just been built. Charlotte had suffered severe bronchitis when only a new-born baby. Martin Gilpin had seen her mother hurrying along St Thomas's Place with her towards the door of the church and he immediately baptized her with some water he always had ready for an emergency, and then told her mother she must take her at once to see a doctor. He didn't mention his reservations about some of these emergency baptisms, and couldn't imagine God damning or even not blessing a child simply because there hadn't been enough time for it.

A little later Charlotte was baptized again at St. Mary's church in Stockport Market Place. Apart from the emergency ones, all baptisms took place here, as there was no font at St Thomas' until 1875. At the second baptism there were godparents present, promises were made, promises that were kept, and Charlotte was brought up a Christian and remained one all her life.

A font was usually kept near the entrance of the church, or 'on the way in' as it would be called. Martin Gilpin had heard of other clergy refusing to baptize a baby until the mother had been cleansed of all her sins, or 'churched' as it used to be called. He felt this was very wrong. It was completely in breach of the Book of Prayer, which stated that anyone at all, at any age, can knock on a minister's door and ask to be baptized, and he would have to do it shortly after. Little did they know that if they were refused they could go to the Bishop and get immediate support.

Charlotte attended Sunday school, and then when she was big enough she had gone to church. She was now 14. She wished they had a Sunday School, maybe even a Sunday College, for teenagers. The school was too young for her and she wanted to be big, but the church was so boring.

She had frequently attended Martin Gilpin's services. She would sit in the gallery upstairs and look down at him in the pulpit, but he didn't often look up at her. She was glad about that. There was a good-looking youth sitting in the gallery opposite her and he would grin and wink at her.

She found out that the boy's name was Rodney. One day she sent him a note via a choirboy taking the collection. It said, 'You seem to smile at me a lot, why don't you come round some time?' and he went round to her house that very day.

'That was very forward of you' said her mother. 'You are supposed to wait until the man asks you.'

'But he was never going to!'

'An Englishman needs time' she said, and she went into some detail about some of the men she'd met from the Continent, mainly Italians. They hadn't needed time.

'Oh, I'd better go to Italy then.'

'You will NOT!'

Next week in church she and the youth sat facing one another in the gallery as they had the week before, but this time he passed her a note. It said, 'Why don't you come outside with me now?'

She looked down at Martin Gilpin so busy giving his sermon; she looked at the door leading out. How easy it would be to slip out and down the stone staircase.

'Excuse me' she said to the woman sitting next to her, 'but I have to go to arrange some flowers.'

'Excuse me' said Rodney to the man sitting next to him 'I have to go to read the next lesson.'

They slipped out on to the landing; no one could see them. Some singing had started up, so no one could hear them. They skipped down the stone stairway laughing and giggling, and ran out of the door into the garden. They hid behind a tree and stayed there until the people started coming out, and then they ran inside a bush, where they were more hidden still. They stayed there until everyone had finished pouring past, then just when they were about to come out, the Reverend Gilpin came out of the church. They both stood there as still and quiet as stone. He walked past, looking straight at the bush almost as though he knew they were there. Then suddenly he turned round and went back inside the church.

'Wow' they both said with their hands on their hearts, 'That was a near miss!'

Next week Gilpin preached in church with great emphasis 'You may deceive man but you will never deceive God,' and according to Charlotte he then looked straight at her. But according to Rodney she just had a guilty conscience.

That was also what some of the girls who came from the mills thought. Charlotte met two of them in church; lots of chances to talk about boys.

After this things got better and better. Rodney taught her to ride a horse. He worked in some stables, so it was easy. It was her dream come true to be able to ride a horse, and more than her dream to be able to have such a teacher.

She had left school at eleven and gone to work for a man called John Jennison. His father, also called John, had been a silk weaver in Macclesfield. In 1815 he built his own home on the corner of Adswood Grove and Stockholme Road. He died in 1825. He passed the house on to his son John, who after the Beer Act in the 1830s turned it into a public house. He called it Adam and Eve. This son had worked for a while at Lawton's Pleasure Gardens, a small one in Portswood.

He began to keep birds and animals at the Adswood home and it wasn't long before he and his wife Maria opened up their little garden to the public. This started just on Sunday afternoons, but as it got busier and busier they opened it up more and more. They employed Charlotte, who was now 15, to serve tea and strawberries, and she became known as the Strawberry Girl.

Charlotte learned a lot. Some people can't take their drink. She once heard someone say, 'That's bad, his breath smells half way through the day time,' and she wondered what the difference was. You shouldn't be drunk any time, night or day. She later discovered what they had meant. It's much more likely to mean that they are drinking more than just socially if it isn't at night.

Strawberry Gardens had stables and offices. Charlotte wished they would employ women in the office because she would get more money. They needed someone like her - she had very good handwriting. But they only employed men. She was also told that there was another reason why she would never get the job. The same thing was happening as had happened to weaving. They were going to get machines to do it.

'Rubbish, how can they do that?' she asked a friend of hers.

'I don't know, but I hear letters of the alphabet are going to be put on to little buttons' said the friend. 'You press the button and it makes a metal letter hit a tape with ink on it, and that goes on to a piece of paper. They are going to be called typewriters.'

Charlotte couldn't imagine it. 'What next?' asked her mother when she told her. She had said so many times before that she didn't know what the world was coming to. They were both well aware that it could mean a lot of people out of work, and they knew what had happened when they had got machines to do the weaving.

Next people started talking about the railway, saying it was going to come to Stockport. She heard they were going to build a couple of railway bridges to go over the railway lines in order to stop people crossing on them. They would be a stone's throw away from Strawberry Gardens. She didn't think it would affect her in any way, until Rodney sent her a poem about it.

> *How would you like to be*
> *Down by the bridge with me?*
> *Oh what I'd give for a moment or two*
> *Under the bridges of Adswood with you*
> *Far from the eyes of night*
> *We would see it so right*
> *Under the bridges of Adswood with you*
> *You'd make my dreams come true.*
> *I'm under the bridge with you*
> *All of my dreams come true.*

It turned out to be all talk about the railways. It would be years before they had any trains, never mind bridges, and then she heard something very bad. John Jennison was moving on with his business. He was going to start up another between Manchester and Hyde and call it Belle Vue. He was going to have a lot more animals there and create a zoo. He offered Charlotte a job and accommodation there. She wanted to know if Rodney could come too. She knew there were some stables he could work in and she had always hoped he would be able to work at Strawberry Gardens. When she was told he couldn't, she turned it down.

She continued to talk endlessly about him and to dream about him. She hoped one day she would be his bride. When she asked the Reverend Gilpin if he would marry them, he laughed and said, 'Wait until he asks you'.

She knew she would have to get another job very quickly, but there was one thing she didn't have to worry about. Her mother was backing her up.

'If you have a real good man, stick to him and don't do anything to risk losing him' she said.

'Looks like I'll be down at the mill though,' Charlotte said, sounding depressed about it. There was one in Stockport only a walk away. There was another at the bottom of Northgate.

She went to singing practice at St Thomas's early one evening, but just as they were finishing a great storm started up. The winds roared at the tower, the windows began to shake and torrents of rain beat against them. It grew very dark; they tried to leave, to struggle home in it, but they had to dash back inside. The trees rocked to and fro and looked as though they were about to fall. Nothing looked safe. They stood at the entrance for a short while, and then, realising it wouldn't soon be over, they went inside the vestry. The Reverend Gilpin had some work to do in any case.

'Looks like we'll be here all night,' said one woman. A girl from the mill whispered into Charlotte's ear, 'A pity you can't be locked up all night in here with Rodney!' and they giggled together.

Chapter Two

LOVE
AND MARRIAGE

There was one thing she and Rodney had in common; neither of them believed in the killing of animals for food, and neither of them ever ate meat or fish. In fact, Rodney had a bit of an argument with a Roman Catholic about it.

'I never eat meat on a Friday, only fish' he said.

'Well fish is meat, so you do eat meat on a Friday.'

'No I don't. I'm a vegetarian every Friday.'

'No you're not. Vegetarians don't eat animals. A fish is an animal that lives in water. If anyone tells you they are a vegetarian and they eat fish, they don't know what a vegetarian is.'

Charlotte said afterwards, 'How can they think a fish is a vegetable?' Then she was told that the word vegetarian didn't come from the word vegetable, but from the Latin for lively. 'We say 'full of beans', don't we?' someone said.

In fact it had been a picture of a dead fish lying on a beach that had first got Rodney and Charlotte talking about it. They found it disgusting. It was supposed to be a pretty picture with a pretty girl in it, yet lying by her side had been this dead animal. You could see its face, and clearly it had been enjoying life shortly before in the water. Why did they kill it? We don't need meat.

Then this Roman Catholic came back to tell them something. He was certain vegetarians were healthier. He had read something about Dr. George Cheyne (1671-1743) and why it was he had this view. There was such a lot to back it up.

'The trouble is,' said Charlotte 'If people believe a thing then they will see it. I get told I look pale.'

'Well,' said the Roman Catholic, 'What did the hypochondriac have written on his grave? 'I kept telling you I wasn't well.' And what will the vegetarian have written on his? 'I kept telling you you should eat meat!"

It isn't that vegetarians lead a healthier life style in other ways; all good scientists have looked into that.

Rodney and Charlotte wondered if they could get a job at the Bible Christian Church in Salford, which was vegetarian. In fact, the minister in charge was talking about starting up a Vegetarian Society. He had looked at a big new house in Altrincham, on the road to Dunham.

'How lovely if it was bought for that, and I could get a job there and accommodation' said Charlotte. She had heard about it; it was surrounded by fields, and people would take their dogs out for walks.

Yet the Bible Christian Church did such a lot of other good things too. It would annoy her when people said, 'You care more about animals than you do for people.' Sometimes it would be someone who hardly knew her. 'Never seen me before, never see me again, how do they know that?' she would ask.

She knew of many cases where the people who did things for animals were also helping people, and so often it was the people who were violent towards animals who were also violent towards human beings.

The pastor, Joseph Brotherton, took over the Bible Christian Church in 1816. He worked hard at making it bigger; he campaigned for the end of child labour and was the first Salford MP to speak out against capital punishment. He also played a large part in opposing slavery. He did much for the welfare of the working classes.

He and his colleagues led the temperance movement, followed by another movement opposing tobacco; there were two temperance pubs in Altrincham in Victorian times and still one in Old Market Place in the 1920s.

Charlotte wished he would do something about flogging. She wouldn't go near Stockport Market if she thought anything like that was going on. It amazed her that some people liked to stand and watch.

The Bible Christian Church also had an office that was open to the public. They could go in and have a look at the books. 'Well that's a library' said Charlotte, wondering if she could get a job there. Why not stay in Stockport and see if she could get something that involved looking after children?

Then she and Rodney started talking about getting married. He was as keen as she was. They wanted to arrange a date. It would be a long way ahead, but she wanted to speak to the Reverend Gilpin about it. He had suffered ill health and gone to stay with his brother, who was a surgeon, and his brother's daughter, Mary Gilpin, who was only fifteen, on the Isle of Man. She planned to speak to him as soon as he came back, but he never did. He died there, at 37. It was a dreadful shock.

Then her mother died. Her good, good mother, she couldn't believe that she would never see her again, and that she would never walk through that door again. Oh how she missed her! How she needed her! She had never known her father, who had died when she was a baby.

A year later the Reverend Henry Bellair, the new pastor, married them. They managed to get lodgings in a small terraced house, a two up, two down, the owner being an elderly woman was away a lot. It was in St Thomas's Place, a side street leading to the church.

Tooty was born a year later. Charlotte found she could still get some money while staying at home looking after her. Girls who worked in the mills often went back to work a few weeks after having a baby. Charlotte would look after it. She would take it to the mill at dinner time for the mother to feed it. After this she would have a dummy dipped into some milk until going-home time, when the mill closed at half past five. The baby seemed content with this, and sometimes Charlotte could feed it herself. She still had plenty of milk. In fact, for a short while she had been a wet nurse for an orphaned baby. At the mill you could always tell which mothers were breast feeding by the damp patches on their overalls.

Something desperately needed doing about the water. It was filthy. Why didn't they? For she couldn't say the ministers in parliament wouldn't put up with it. They must know about the problem - the River Thames stank, and it was just outside the House of Commons.

Something also needed doing about sanitation. With tears in her eyes she remembered happy days when talking about toilets, privies as they were called in those days, and you would be lucky if you had one of your own. They were so often shared among families and always kept outside. Rodney said, 'They're going to stop that. They're going to start bringing them inside, and every house will have one.'

She had heard other people say this, and comment 'How dirty to have a toilet inside.'

'Don't be so disgusting,' she told Rodney as he stood there grinning all over his face. He then made another couple of jokes about it. 'Oh you are vulgar, what a vulgar mind you've got!' She told him. His mother was washing some dishes nearby and joined in.

'Men are like that, they've all got disgusting minds, and I don't trust any of them' she said.

'Well I don't trust some of these women' said Charlotte as she thought about some of the girls from the mill. 'I don't know how you differentiate.'

Yet it wasn't only the girls at the mill who could be disgusting. She remembered what one of them had told her. She had worked on a yacht and a Lady Summers was being interviewed by the committee for the second time about bad language. Some of the girls that had worked in factories or in a mill were also working on the yacht but they were all right, there had been no complaints about them, it was Lady Summers who was in trouble.

Now she had to think very seriously about everything. The drinking water was still awful. In many places there was only one standpipe for the whole street, which was turned on for an hour and pumped untreated into the nearest river. The poor had to go with their buckets and pans, and sometimes when it looked clean it wasn't. It wasn't safe to drink.

But their happiness was not to last. Rodney fell ill. He started developing black blotches on the skin, choking and vomiting, and Charlotte was well aware of what this could mean. 'Oh no!' She cried, but there was nothing anyone could do. It was cholera, and he was dead within a few days.

She walked about in a state of disbelief. His death brought back the loss of her mother all over again. People told her, 'Oh, it can do that to you, even the death of a pet can make you grieve all over again for an earlier bereavement.' She thought she saw her mother across the road, although it was only someone that looked like her, and then a horse and carriage got in the way. 'Oh go away, go away!' she had wanted to cry out at them, as though they were wrecking her one chance of seeing her mother again.

Christmas was coming, and everyone wanted to celebrate the birth of Christ by spreading goodwill. Charlotte did not. She wanted to run away to a place where she could cry and no one could see her. She thought it very strange that all through this dreadful nightmare of Rodney being so ill, she had hardly cried once.

Then in a dream he came back. In the dream it had all only happened in a terrible nightmare and she was telling him all about it.

It was just after the time the first Christmas cards had come out in 1843, and very soon they became popular with the penny post. In those days postmen delivered on Christmas Day. The day would traditionally be celebrated by having a goose, followed by plum pudding, although it would be mainly the wealthy that enjoyed such things. They would be waited on by servants, who would not get a day off on Christmas Day.

The poor were talking about getting a goose club somewhere they could put their money into every week, to save up for Christmas. It made Charlotte feel sick. She had been in Alexandra Park, in Edgeley, watching them playing so happily around the ponds. If only they would leave them alone.

Queen Victoria's husband, Prince Albert, first introduced the Christmas tree from his own country, Germany. They were decorated with nuts, sweets and presents. Holly, ivy, and mistletoe were used to decorate the rest of the room.

A well-meaning couple invited her round, but this made her worse because she saw how life should be. It made her feel guilty that seeing a couple so happy together could make her feel so miserable. When she heard that someone else had had a similar experience, she felt that more should be done for the bereaved. People should know more about it. When Martin Gilpin had died his mother had been devastated, and died herself within six months. Some people felt there was a connection. One person said, 'It's as though they already have a growth and a bereavement triggers it off.'

This couple offered her some goose and then remembered she was a vegetarian. They weren't rich and they weren't poor; they had a Christmas tree and decorated the room as best they could.

A week later the woman came round again and invited her to her home once more. She said, 'There will be nobody else in the house'. Had someone told her? She went on to say 'I have crushed some nuts and mixed them up with other things, I have made a roast nut bake'

Charlotte went. As they ate it together, followed by plum pie, they talked about Martin Gilpin and his mother. This woman knew someone else the same thing had happened to.

'In that case the one that died was very old' she said. 'They had been ill for some time. I think people made the assumption that it didn't matter much, a relative wouldn't be upset if it's someone that's old, and yet it can matter dreadfully.'

There was one thing Charlotte felt confident about; she had always done her best for her husband. She had met other people who only thought about what they had done wrong.

'You should think about all the things you did right' she would say to them. They were beating themselves up. One woman could only think about the last night of her husband's life. He had wanted them to go to a concert together and she had refused.

'No chance,' she had told him, putting her feet up on a stool. 'I've been teaching kids all day and I'm having an early night tonight.' She found it hard to forgive herself.

Charlotte told her that if it had been the other way round, if she had suddenly died, then he would have been saying, 'How selfish of me to expect her to go to a show, I should have been telling her to keep her feet up and making her a cup of tea.'

Charlotte was concerned about what a loss it had been for Tooty. She no longer had a father; in fact she had lost a very good one. He'd had a job, earned enough money to keep them both, and he had done it with so much love. He had adored his little girl.

But most of all she thought about Rodney. She felt resentful. Why should a good man like him be cheated of his life? He had fought hard to keep it. He hadn't wanted to die. She also felt resentful about some of the bad people who go on and on living. She wondered if it was the evil that kept them going. One person said to her about the ones that were good, 'We wonder how we will manage now that they have gone, and we don't manage. Things go wrong that wouldn't have happened if they'd be there.' Others would tell her she had no right to judge, it was up to the Good Lord to say when one should be taken away, and she felt like slapping them across the face.

She realised that they were right; we can't go along judging who should live and who should die. But she found it very difficult to take.

There was another thing which troubled her very much. She felt that she would have been able to accept it, to live again, it if he had left her. She said it again and again and to everyone she met, 'If he was being very naughty, like living in London with some other woman, it would be completely different, but I just can't take this. I cannot accept that he is dead.'

Now she was in the workhouse. While there she attended St Thomas's Church three times on Sunday, but she rarely stayed for the whole of the service. It was too much. She knew only too well how to slip down the stone staircase and into the garden, but this time it wasn't with him in joy, it was to cry, alone. A lot of people saw her go and felt it better to leave her. They didn't know what to do. If it isn't one thing it's another. There had been so much trouble because people just don't care, but this wasn't the case here. People were very sorry and frustrated because they wanted to help, but they just did not know how to go about it. They knew nothing about helping the bereaved.

She leaned against a gravestone and could only see gloom and clouds ahead. Then suddenly, Rodney was standing there. His face was full of compassion. He seemed to be telling her, 'Don't cry for me.'

'I cry for you all of the time' She told him.

He remained there for another half minute looking compassionately on; she knew he had got her message. After this she knew she had to get over it. She had to accept it, he had gone and he was never coming back.

She knew it was worse to lose your husband when you are old. At least she was still young. In fact she remembered something that Elizabeth Isherwood, the daughter-in-law of the Reverend Bellair, had said to her. She had just married his son in Marple. She said, 'I can't imagine what it would be like should anything happen to him now. Whatever can it be like for people who are old?'

Next morning she had to get up early to work in the laundry. Through eyes sore with crying, she could see the sky. There wasn't a cloud in the heavens. There was a clear glow of crimson and scarlet together. She wondered if this was to tell her that Rodney was happy somewhere else.

But on this day, the day of the riot at the workhouse, things were very different. She went rushing through the door of St Thomas'. Henry Bellair was sitting at the entrance with his daughter-in-law Elizabeth and another man. She knew Elizabeth well. So many of the gentry would be stand-offish, but she would have a friendly air about her. Gently the Reverend asked her, 'What is it?'

'They have taken my dress!' she howled. It was a dress she'd hidden away for when she came out, for when she no longer had to wear a uniform. She had indeed fought for it with words, while old Hilda, for she was very old, had fought for it with her hands. Then a young woman joined in the struggle. Still clinging to Tooty, Charlotte had shouted at them, 'Give it back, give it back!'

Then more rioters came into the room, and things got really out of hand. She soon realised she had to give in - they were going to take it. It was heartbreaking seeing them walking out of the door with it. Yet she was so thankful that she still had Tooty. Her daughter was far more precious than any dress.

Hilda was still very upset. She'd been very mixed up in the struggle and felt so defeated. 'I don't think of myself as old,' she told Charlotte, 'I think I'm still young.' She had been a governess at the workhouse until she'd gone so deaf she could only hear with an ear trumpet. She was so frail. Oh why couldn't she live outside! There was such a thing as outdoor relief, and she was the sort of person that got it.

'Why don't they rob the rich?' Charlotte asked the Reverend Bellair, for they had taken bread as well as clothes. 'If they are going to break in anywhere they should take some dresses and bread out of these big houses and bring them to us in the workhouse.'

She did not realise that she had made a very important point there. It was something that was worrying a lot of people. Henry Bellair was not the only one who feared a revolution like the one in France of 1789. How well his parents remembered that - they had talked about it as though it was yesterday, and at times he had felt he was there.

He felt so much for Charlotte. How terrifying it must have been to have all those people descend upon her. He thought about Marie Antoinette, the Queen of France, who had seen it all from her window, the crowd getting bigger and bigger, and then they started marching towards the palace. It was like a horrific nightmare. They got nearer and nearer until they were in the palace grounds, then they were in the palace. Then she could hear them coming up the stairs. The door was locked, but it soon started to rattle and break down as they got inside to get her. She stood there terrified, and the next thing she knew they were taking her away.

Would people ever forgive the Queen? She had known what was going on. When she was told her people were crying from hunger because they had no bread, she was said to have replied, 'Why don't they eat cake?' Henry was certain that this had been contempt, not just ignorance. He had heard some sick jokes himself made by some of the rich about the poor. At times he felt that they knew no better.

Henry wanted people to be better educated. He had considered leaving the church for a while and working with schools - maybe become a school inspector.

'The answer to your question is very deep' he told Charlotte. 'But please don't think I haven't thought about it already. I think about it a lot. I think about what little I can do. No one can do everything, but everybody can do something.'

He was glad she had brought up the subject of forgiveness. 'How can you preach about such things, why should you forgive?' she had asked. 'They're not sorry for what they have done. They would gladly do it again.'

'To know all is to forgive all, and people who bear resentment are unhappy people' replied Henry. 'Hatred breeds hatred.'

'But getting revenge isn't the same thing as fighting for justice. People have got to be punished for what they have done. Some Protestants and Catholics have been absolutely hateful to one another, burning each other at the stake!'

Henry didn't argue. He prayed to God for guidance, knowing these were dangerous times and he could only do his best.

Then the conversation became more jovial and she cheered up. They talked about better days ahead.

He suddenly remembered some cake someone had given him for anyone who needed it. He took it out of a drawer. He knew that she knew the story of Marie Antoinette.

'Have some of this, it was given me by someone rich' he said.

The four of them laughed together. It was now getting late. They walked back to the workhouse, Charlotte still carrying Tooty. Everywhere was now quiet. Many arrests had been made, but the riot had far from gone away. It had merely moved on. Charlotte slipped into bed and went into a deep sleep.

* * * * * * * * *

The next morning the Reverend Bellair visited a Mrs Mares with his daughter-in-law Elizabeth. He told her about his discussion with Charlotte the day before. Mrs Mares found a dress for Charlotte and said she would speak to her about it in church. Maybe she would like her to keep it somewhere safe for when she came out.

Her heart was full of compassion. She wished she could do more, but it was very difficult. She gave regularly to the poor. They kept a record of it all in the poor book in church, things like shoes and weaving wheels.

Henry stayed a while and they talked for a long time. In some ways things had progressed. He remembered a diary written by his great grandfather Jacob, which contained details about the family going back many years, and revealed that Jacob and his father had been upset at the way women used to be treated. They even burned some of them at the stake as witches. He made mention of this to Mrs Mares and then realised he was greatly upsetting her. He tried to change the subject, but she wouldn't let him.

'I have to tell you, my father was a hateful man' she said. 'He would talk about how he hated these women. He would call them evil, and say that the only way to get rid of evil was to burn it. 'Burn them, burn them!' he would say. They would also burn their cats. I don't know why he hated them so much, he didn't hate all women, but when he did it was for no apparent reason.'

Henry Bellair thought of some of his parishioners who had been upset by more recent things that had gone on, and realised that people depended on him as pastor of the church. He couldn't be weak. He had to be the strong one, the one to say something soothing, though he didn't always feel strong himself. He talked to Mrs Mares about it, because he found her very supportive. He wondered if there were more women-haters around than people realised. Mrs Mares wondered it too. Some people would say it wasn't hate but wanting control, but when they were being so aggressive it couldn't be called anything else.

Mrs Mares went on, 'Knocking their wives about, they seem to want to have something to complain about. They can only see evil in the woman, they blame her for the least little thing and at times it's as though they want things to go wrong so that they can say it's her, so they can take charge. I sometimes wonder if this is the case with some of these powerful rulers.'

Henry Bellair remembered something he had read in his great grandfather's diary. When leading a woman to the stake to be burned as a witch, the men would make her wear a mask to make her look grotesque, like some monster from space. It was enough to frighten anyone. Why did they want to do that? And why do some men want to believe wildly unfair things about their wives? It must be to justify what they were doing.

Henry knew that some women were dreadful, but in his experience it wasn't they who had violent husbands. He felt at times as some of his family had felt in history, that there was no light at the end of the tunnel.

'Why do they marry them in the first place?' he asked her.

'Because they need her. They can't manage the combination of their need for her with their fear of her.'

They both agreed it was happening across the classes. A lot of people thought it only went on in slums and among the uneducated or badly brought up, but this was not necessarily true. It happens because a man has seen how his father has treated his mother and considered it the norm. Yet quite a few people strongly disagreed, saying that in their experiences this wasn't the case. Sometimes a woman of class has more to lose, not only financially, and so is afraid to report it. She may feel it is a disgrace for her to have to admit to this, or she may fear that no one will believe her.

'There's no cure for it,' said Mrs Mares 'He won't find out with time that she's not evil.'

'I know' said Henry. 'A lot of people think that underneath it all he loves her really and this will show up in a crisis, but it won't. In a crisis she will find out more than ever that there is no feeling there for her, and that it is disastrous to be married to him.'

'I wish they'd let women work in offices' Mrs Mares said. 'It would give them more independence. For example, arithmetic. A woman can do that every bit as well as a man, but if it's the man that gets the wages, then it's the man that has control of the money and that means he's got control of her life.'

Henry Bellair thought about it. He realised it would make it easier to give men the jobs as they don't have to give up work to have babies. He knew his parents had never had any trouble, that his father had always provided, but he also knew all men were not the same. Some will abuse it and some women will wake up every morning with a cloud of fear over them. They will go to bed at night with the same fear, wondering how they are going to get some housekeeping money.

They also talked about what absolute idiots these men think their wives are. One woman had said to Mrs Mares, 'It's an ordinary fool who doesn't see a doctor soon enough if she has a cough, but a complete idiot who doesn't take a child to see a doctor when it's spitting up blood.' She was thinking of a Lady Martin. Yet it had been another woman she'd been talking about, not a man; it was her mother in law. She had asked her if her child was doing this, as though Lady Martin wouldn't know it was a real emergency, and of course the child must see a doctor, especially as spitting up blood is a symptom of tuberculosis.

Mrs Mares had thought it was basically the same as some of these men - treating someone as a complete idiot in order to get control.

She and Henry went on to talk about voting, and how wrong it was that only gentlemen had the vote. His father had been lucky enough to get a vote. Henry felt more determined than ever to build good schools so that everyone could learn to read and write. He knew that if you catch children when they are very young they will learn. He also knew that some of the people setting up schools hadn't a clue how to teach. He wanted them to be trained.

They talked at length about their fears that there was going to be a civil war in America to free the slaves. They prayed together that many lives would not be lost. They both knew people who had been there and seen what was happening. They knew one man who had helped a slave escape and get across the sea to Liverpool, where he was safe. It was obvious by looking at him that he was mixed race. Things like that made people believe it when they said the masters were interfering with the girls.

Joseph Barker and Joseph Moore of Hale spoke eloquently against slavery before it was abolished in 1833. Two former slaves, Henry 'Box' Brown and Samuel Alexander 'Boxer' Smith, toured England in the 1850s campaigning against slavery and they stayed with Moore. Smith had bought his freedom and had smuggled Brown out of slavery in a box.

Both Henry and Mrs Mares knew some progress had been made against slavery, but they were surprised at what was still allowed. They weren't sure what laws had been passed, or if they had been enforced. They just knew people had been campaigning for years to stop slaves being flogged or chained, or having their children sold.

He had heard one sad story at first hand, of a 13-year-old girl who would probably never see her mother again. Everyone had pleaded with the owner not to sell her. They tried to keep track of where she was, but it took some doing, and then they sold the mother. How would they be able to find one another again, even if they were one day all freed?

Henry knew someone who was prepared to give his life to the campaign against slavery. 'If you get killed in a war, think of the loss that will be to everyone and how a good man like you is needed for other reforms,' he said, but he had another point, for he was no pacifist. He feared that if slaves were freed by fighting and killing instead of by steady progress, it would finish up with a lot more resentment and create a very big race problem for years to come.

Yet he could understand why people couldn't wait. He knew he wouldn't if he were a slave. He also knew that laws and church rules were not kept, and that the fact that something was against the law didn't mean it wasn't going on. Like many people, he wondered just how bad these wars were going to get with all the new weapons they were inventing.

He walked home in a very thoughtful mood. Charlotte had got him thinking deeply, but at least he had managed to get another dress for her.

Many years later he read what a young clergyman had written: 'This evening being May Eve I ought to have put some birch and witan (mountain ash) over the door to keep out the old witch but I was too lazy to go out and get it. Let us hope the old witch will not come in during the night. The young witches are very welcome.' (Francis Kilvert's diary, last published by Book Club Association)

It was very naughty of him to say that only young witches were welcome inside his home, but the fact that he could be so frivolous about it did show that it was all history to him. Henry hoped this would mean that all bad things do eventually come to an end.

He picked up his great grandfather's diary and read parts of it. As he did so he began to nod off. He felt as though he was there, and began to dream. He saw his great-great grandfather, Isaac. Isaac had been haunted for the rest of his life by seeing women burned at the stake as witches, and his son Jacob had tried so hard to comfort him. 'Dad, you did so much towards getting that stopped, please only think of that' he would say.

Isaac had thought it was a nightmare that would never end. When only fifteen he had once rushed towards them as they were about to burn a witch, shouting, 'Stop doing that! Don't burn that woman!'

The poor woman had been tied up high on a stake on the village green. Shortly she would be set alight, but other people held him back. 'Take care,' they said, 'some of the people in the crowd here are real thugs.'

But he didn't take care about the consequences. As the woman was being led down the street through the jeering mob, he kept shouting 'Stop!'

He would cry with helplessness. He was so frustrated. 'Another poor wretched soul has gone' he would say as he walked away. He could never understand why so often they seemed to be sympathetic towards him, because it upset him so much, yet showed no pity for the woman. Nor could he understand why they would sometimes make her wear such a ghastly mask. They wanted her to be ugly. Why?

'No one can do everything' Jacob would tell him. 'Everybody can do something, and you did plenty towards getting it stopped.' It upset him to see his father so upset and feeling helpless, for to Jacob he had always been the strong one, the one he had always looked up to and depended upon, the one who knew the answer to everything. Yet at times he saw him cry like a baby.

'Do you know, Jacob' he would go on, 'They said prayers before they burned her and said at the same time that she worshipped the devil. Who did they think they were worshipping when they were doing that?'

'Oh Dad, you must know you have a place waiting for you in heaven, and meanwhile you must enjoy life on earth, put all this behind you, those days have gone' said Jacob.

Now it was Jacob who had to be the strong one, the one to say something soothing to his father. Yet he didn't always feel strong himself.

Henry Bellair woke up with a jolt. The fire had long gone out. He was still sitting in the armchair. He had slept some time, it was almost morning and he knew another day would shortly be ahead of him. This dream had made him feel strong again.

Chapter Three

BOWDON

Charlotte reached the house she was looking for and walked up the drive, hoping no one would come out and ask her what she wanted. The smoke coming from the chimney looked welcoming and comforting, and so different from the smoke in the slums. There were too many chimneys there.

She couldn't stay feeling comfortable for long. The front door was at the side, up some steps. It looked enormous and daunting. She walked past it, round to the back and into the back yard. Gloria had explained it all to her, how she would find it.

Then she saw her in the scullery and knocked on the window. Gloria rushed out to greet her.

'I am so glad to see you, come in!' she said.

Gloria was 40 and had been a friend of the family for years. She had known both her parents well and had gone to Charlotte's wedding. They had quite a bit in common.

They sat and chatted in the kitchen for a while and Tooty and Charlotte tucked into the food. There had been a dinner party the night before, and plenty of food was left over. None of them could understand why the food in the workhouse was so bad - they lived largely on gruel. Yet people knew something about good nourishment and they knew no one was going to do well on that alone. Porridge was drunk straight out of the bowl and food eaten with bare hands, as there would be no cutlery. The Poor Act 1834 allowed them to insist that they had their rations weighed, but who would dare stick up for such a right?

The staff were automatically loathed, and it was very unfair that the workhouse master's daughter had been shouted at on her way home from school. She seemed such a timid little soul. Everything was very different from the way it had been intended.

Ironically the man who first started up the workhouse, with good intentions, was called Mr Carey. He wanted to improve diet and nourishment and teach girls to spin so they would have a trade. In the early 1700s John Carey had been full of optimism, sometimes justified, feeling confident that old and poor people could now live in comfort. But more than anything else he wanted to give more outdoor relief.

The good nourishment he talked about was bread, cheese, peas, turnips, porridge, carrots, potatoes and beef. Beef was considered a luxury, but Charlotte found it revolting. People would sometimes talk to her about it, not realising it sounded obscene to her.

She made mention to Gloria of the goat she had seen across the way.

'Oh, they're pets' said Gloria. 'They're not bred for milk. A lot of people don't like them. They've been chewing tree bark and they've even eaten someone's washing!'

Charlotte was well aware that goats can be a dreadful nuisance, as well as taking up a lot of land and drinking a great deal of water. She had heard it said that while some people grow fruit trees to help people, others breed goats that destroy them.

They went back to talking about the workhouses. Gloria said, 'It seems the first person who thought a workhouse should be a deterrent, not a place of comfort, was a country gentleman called Mathew Marryott.'

'Oh Gloria, you do know your history,' said Charlotte, determined to make certain it soon would be all history to her and Tooty.

They went down into the cellar, where there was a glorious fire burning. A couple of beds were there for Charlotte and Tooty.

'I'll just say I've got friends in should Mr or Mrs Carlton ask me anything' said Gloria. 'They've seen me with plenty of them about.' Yet she doubted they would ask. She had worked there some time, they depended on her and they trusted her. They had had such trouble with unreliable staff before. And they rarely came into the kitchen.

Above the kitchen door was a row of bells for Mr and Mrs Carlton to ring if they wanted anything. Gloria liked it that way. She didn't want them in the kitchen, she wanted it to herself. Also living in the house were their two young sons, Winston and Samuel, aged 18 and 16, but they were usually away at boarding school.

It was almost as though they had separate flats. The kitchen and scullery were on a floor of their own with a small lobby. The cellar steps led out of this lobby. There were then two more stairs next to it which led into the hall and the rest of the house. It was sometimes known as the House of Stairs for this reason. There seemed to be endless banisters going up and up and round and round, enough to make anyone go giddy if they looked at them too long.

Gloria and Charlotte settled down in the cellar in front of the log fire to talk. 'The Carltons won't have anything else but a log fire because of all this trouble with soot catching fire in the chimneys' said Gloria. 'No one goes up a chimney here, they come round with a brush on the end of a long rod'.

Charlotte hoped this would solve it. In any case, should a modern house like this have a lot of problems? She didn't know how right she was. Even as far back as 1834 there had been building regulations relating to the construction of chimneys. They went on to talk about other things, but just as they were about to go into something deep a bell went. 'Got to go!' said Gloria, dashing off.

Charlotte settled down into bed. Somehow she felt things were going to turn out fine.

* * * * * * * * *

Jacqueline Everett walked up Sandy Lane. She had been visiting an old pal of hers, Margaret Wheetman, a widow of 65 who lived at the bottom of Sandy Lane in a very big house called Holly Bank. She would have different servants living in the house from time to time.

Margaret Wheetman was talking about her nephew Edmund, who had just finished his training to be a doctor in London. He had planned on having a wonderful future there, only to find himself back again in Bowdon with his parents. There had been a dreadful outbreak in Altrincham of cholera and dysentery. Edmund felt duty started at home, and this was where he was needed.

A lot of people were working hard to battle the epidemic, including health inspectors, and especially down a narrow lane called Chapel Walk, later to be called Regent Road, and the side streets off it. The manure was piled up high and the sanitation was very bad in all the houses.

Edmund may have been most influenced by the case of Emily, a young servant girl, and Mrs Samuels, the woman she worked for. They had been living happily in a three-bedroomed house in Altrincham. They could get enough water for what they wanted, and had been able to deal with the sanitation all right; it wasn't in a place which was too overcrowded. Mrs Samuels had been persuaded to take in Emily from the workhouse on being told how the poor girl had been orphaned, though she hadn't really wanted her. She started finding it extremely trying, as she liked to have the house to herself and wanted to be on her own again.

Yet Emily was a good girl. She was 11 years old when she first came, worked hard when there was a lot to do and took it easy when she could. Now she was 14. Mrs Samuels discussed the problem with her friends.

'I hate doing it' she said. 'I can't chuck her out, but I can't be tied to her for the rest of my life.'

'Hang on a bit' they told her, 'you may find she's telling you she's going, but if not, see if you can find her somewhere else in Bowdon. Tell her she can come back if things go wrong.'

They even talked about her going to London eventually. They said that as she was happy in service there should be plenty of jobs and accommodation for her there. The girl had wings. One thing was certain, she was to be assured that she would not have to go back to the workhouse; too many people would be keeping an eye on her. That was one good thing the workhouse had done for her. It had made certain she could read and write absolutely fluently, and now that there was the penny post she would soon be able to let anyone know how she was getting on.

Mrs Samuels kept putting off telling her to do this, and things went on the same as usual in the place Emily considered her home. It was a home she very much deserved to have.

That was until one Monday afternoon. Mrs Samuels came in and couldn't find her. She stood at the bottom of the stairs calling her, and when she didn't come she thought she had popped out somewhere, as she did sometimes, as she was not kept to a strict timetable. But as time went by and Emily still didn't appear, Mrs Samuel started getting more concerned. Eventually she went up to her room and found her lying ill on her bed.

'I feel so ill, I feel absolutely dreadful' said Emily. The doctor was brought in immediately and Emily was taken at once to a sanatorium, but two days later the poor girl was dead with dysentery.

Mrs Samuels was devastated. She was glad she had never let Emily know she was planning on asking her to go. She walked about the house feeling bewildered, for it was now so empty and bare. She thought about Emily endlessly, wishing she could have one more moment alone with her to tell her she could stay as long as she liked.

Mrs Everett continued on her way up Sandy Lane. She could see Spring Bank House in the distance and all the land that went with it. 'What do they want all that for?' she wondered. She passed four terraced houses on the opposite side of the road, built specially for the workers of Holly Bank. She passed the home of a man who was campaigning to stop chimney sweeps sending boys up chimneys. He was finding it needed a lot of perseverance.

This was a cause she too felt strongly about, but for now she could only think about herself. She was hungry and looking forward to her supper. She hoped the girls would have it ready for her when she got in. She was used to servants. Her young niece, Alice, had just left boarding school and had criticized her about it.

'You should be doing something about the poor' she said.

'Can't I do anything right?' she replied.

For she had got a girl from out of the workhouse. She was all right, a good worker, yet she had felt she didn't need anyone else; she had already got one person. She'd been nagged into it.

Her leg began to play up as she continued on her way up the hill. She was 61, old age was creeping in, and she had a touch of arthritis. But what was this? There were police everywhere. People were pouring down the lane, out of the Griffin at the top of the lane, coming out of their houses, they were coming from everywhere.

She asked a passer-by what had happened.

'A prostitute's been found murdered at the back of Spring Bank!' she said.

'A prostitute, in Bowdon?'

The murdered girl was the second in two months. Spring Bank

was the name of the garden belonging to the house of the same name. There was a passageway leading along the back of it, and it was in this alleyway that both victims been found.

A servant girl shouted from an upstairs window, 'There's going to be another bloody revolution like the one in France if nothing is done about this poverty!'

'Consider me put in my place!' she shouted back, and the girl laughed. It was a private joke between them. She was a girl like Alice; it gave her a buzz to give cheek to her elders, but Mrs Everett was fast becoming an old woman and learning how to answer back.

'I take pleasure in giving cheek to my youngers!' she shouted back, and the girl laughed again before putting the window down.

The woman the girl worked for leaned out of another upstairs window and demanded to know what the servant girl had said.

'Oh she was just saying how pretty those flowers were over there' said Mrs Everett, pointing at some nearby. She knew that the woman was a great believer in keeping the workers in their place and considered that Mrs Everett should be a comrade of hers in this, but Mrs Everett was careful not to say anything that would cause trouble for the girl.

Then she saw her nephew David walking up the road ahead of her and turning left into South Road. She was pleased to see him. He was her brother's son and she had helped bring him up. He was doing well. He had just qualified as a solicitor and was working for a firm in Stockport.

* * * * * * * * *

Mrs Everett knew more about the French Revolution than anyone in England could possibly have imagined, because she had been born right there in France during the Revolution, in the palace at Versailles. Her mother Françoise had told her all about it. In fact her

43

mother had been terrified at one time, thinking that the revolutionaries might come in there and then, raid the place while she was still in labour and kill both her and her baby. Little Jacqueline had been born during a major disturbance. Françoise heard it all.

Things had happened to make Mrs Everett far more afraid of people who were stupid than those who were nasty. She was not to know in those far-off days that in a hundred years' time she would have a great-great-great niece who would have very much agreed with her. It was a shame they could never meet.

In 1950 this niece was a diabetic, and she had dreadful trouble with people who did not accept her condition. They wouldn't have it that she had to keep to her diet. They would say to her 'There's no sugar in these scones' although of course there was. She would say, 'You'll find out when I wake up in the ambulance that there was plenty of sugar.'

But now it was 1850 and Mrs Everett knew so much less about it, apart from what her mother had told her. In 1789, on the day she was born, Françoise, absolutely exhausted with it all, had laid her on her chest. She could hear her husband Jacques talking.

'We've got to move out of here fast, I'm not messing about any longer!' he said.

'What a time to choose!' Françoise cried out to him, feeling too exhausted even to roll over in bed. 'Please let me have another day of rest!'

Even after all the noise had quietened down, she still found herself jumping at the slightest sound and looking nervously around, as though to say, 'Who heard that?'

Jacques and Françoise had lived in Paris a long time. They did try to do something about the poor, but it was very difficult. If you helped one of them they'd all be round and there was so much more to it than just handing out food or money. It wouldn't always be the needy that came.

It would sometimes be the scroungers. You couldn't get rid of them and you would be afraid of what revenge they might seek if you didn't give in to their impossible demands. Sometimes they had considered hiding away somewhere and pretending to be poor themselves.

One night Jacques had been deciding what to have for supper that night when he noticed a hungry face looking in through the window. He would gladly have gone out into the garden, invited him in and offered him a feast, but it wasn't that easy. He didn't dare. It was this that made him say for the first time 'We've got to get out of this place'. He knew that the face at the window wasn't going to put up with his hunger for ever. Eventually, if he was starved long enough, he would revolt.

Yet they continued to be visitors at the palace. Jacques had planned to go to England before Jacqueline was born, not after. He knew that Marie Antoinette, the Queen of France, was an absolute fool. They could not get her to understand how serious the situation was becoming. She dismissed it as nonsense when one lady arrived at the palace quite traumatized because a large stone had been thrown at her carriage.

She also let it get out that she had bought a very expensive necklace.

'Do you have to have it?' someone had asked her impatiently. It was their head they were thinking of, not hers. They were a lot more worried about it when she wouldn't keep quiet about it. 'She's no ordinary fool, she's an extraordinary fool,' Jacqueline's father had said.

A couple of weeks before, one of the men from the palace stables had been in the centre of Paris and was horrified by what he saw. It had made his blood run cold. A man was standing on a soap box giving a speech about Marie Antoinette. There was so much hatred in his eyes and his words that the man knew he would gladly kill the Queen.

He went back to the palace very motivated. He went towards

Marie Antoinette's room, a place where a commoner should never be, but there was no stopping him. He met her on the stairs and in no uncertain terms he told her, 'Get out of here before they come and kill you!'

He couldn't even begin to get the Queen to take the situation seriously. Someone else did – Jacques. He was very serious. He felt very threatened that the Queen was such a fool, and even more so when she would start to make a fuss about something that didn't matter. He and the commoner spoke together about it in a way a commoner and gentleman would never normally do. All barriers were breaking down. Exchanging very few words, especially when talking about the necklace, they would use slang and blasphemy and say things like, 'Is there anything she can keep her great big gob shut about?'

They wondered if they could kill her. If she was out of the way they might be able to prevent a revolution. She had stood in the way with so many things. Their talk was hypothetical, yet at times it was becoming more realistic. After all, who would be sorry about her loss? There were plenty of people who wouldn't want to know. How big an investigation would there be into it, and how corrupt would it be? They would talk it over. It would be so easily believed, with all the hatred about, that someone in the mob had done it, not necessarily to a plan.

Maybe they could find a way of getting her out of the carriage, say it had broken down, get it to go where no one could see them and then kill her with a big stone. Everyone would say it had been thrown by someone in the crowd.

They thought about it a lot. The problem was, how would they manage it without endangering the coachmen? It would be impossible to do it without involving them. Would it be possible to fake some 'mistake'?

Their plans started getting more realistic. They even began to plan on a place and a time, but there was something that mattered much more than that. Marie Antoinette continued to be thoroughly dangerous. She was a dangerous fool, and she was frightening them into murder.

In the end they decided to drop it all. It would involve too many people, and when too many people know, these things get found out. It was decided that each of them should look after themselves, and that they could only do that by escaping.

Jacqueline's father made arrangements for money to be transferred into a bank in England and sent his other son, his wife and Jacqueline ahead of him. He never joined them - it was too late. Jacques went to the guillotine.

Françoise lived in fear ever after. She didn't even like having a lot of money. She kept it hidden away, and for much of her life she lived a lie.

It is difficult for anyone who has lived through such an era to accept that the old days have gone, and in any case, a lot of people weren't sure they really had. Like many people, Jacqueline's mother had reason to believe that a revolution in England might follow.

Françoise lived in West Road in Bowdon and kept Jacqueline educated. She made certain she knew the risks of poverty. 'If you keep people very poor they will revolt' she would say. She also made certain that French was her first language. She would say to her, 'Do your best to teach it to people. It's in our interests that they are educated.'

Jacqueline and her mother also had hearts. They didn't like to see people poor and deprived.

Chapter Four

DAVID

It was Sunday when Charlotte walked up the hill with Tooty. She had seen the tower of Bowdon Church, so she knew the way. The bells were ringing, which told her there was going to be a service.

She turned left at the top and there it was. She went in through the door at the back and saw that the procession was about to start down the aisle, so she slipped up a spiral stone staircase on the right, so that no one would see her. She thought it would lead to a balcony. It did; it also led to the belfry, and shortly afterwards the bellringers came down to join them.

Tooty wasn't used to bells in a church. She felt she was sitting with some very important people. She couldn't sit still, she was so excited.

Charlotte looked around the church and saw that someone had hung a framed verse on the wall about the bellringers.

The Ringers' Orders
You ringers all, observe these orders well
He pays his sixpence that o'erturns the bell
And he that rings with either spur or hat
Must pay his sixpence certainly for that
And he that rings and does disturb the peal
Must pay his sixpence or a gun of ale

These laws elsewhere in every church are used
That bells and ringers must not be abused.

After the service they walked a long way round back to the house. They went down some stone steps in the church garden at the side of the church and found themselves facing a small police station. Then they went down a lane called Church Brow. They went past a house on one side which would later become the vicarage, and some thatched cottages on the other. Charlotte looked at them and said, 'That's the place where I would like to live.'

As she turned into East Downs Road she could hear some disturbance going on along the road. She was curious and went to have a look. Two gentlemen were having an argument. She hid behind a bush in the next door garden and Tooty climbed up a tree to see better. Whatever could it be?

Then suddenly it clicked. It was an argument about chimney sweeps.

'You had a climbing boy up your chimney!' said one.

'I didn't!' said the second.

'I'll bring a private prosecution against you if you don't stop it, and I am watching you!'

'And we're watching you too' Charlotte muttered under her breath. Then Tooty shouted it out loud and across to them. Charlotte stretched her hand up to slap her and tell her to stop it, but neither of the men heard. Either that or they were too engaged in their dispute to pick it up.

'It's not against the law!' shrieked one to drown the noise.

'It is if he's under 21,' said the other, as a woman came out of the house to take the dog in.

'Oh really!' He asked sarcastically, 'since when?'

'Since 1840.'

The other started speaking more quietly, as though to try to reason with him. 'Now look here, will you? I just ask a master sweep to send someone round to clean my chimney. How am I to know who he'll send or how they work?'

'Common sense.'

'He was a proper apprentice of a master sweep.'

'Oh, you do know who he was?'

'Speak to the master sweep about it'

'I have done.'

The voices started to get loud again. 'Very coincidental that you got him so very quickly after a young boy had been roaming Bowdon early in the morning crying out, 'Soot-oh-sweep.' Are you sure you got him from a master sweep?'

'Yes.'

'Well why you won't tell me his name?'

'You said you had already spoken to him about it.'

'I have spoken to all the master sweeps.'

'And it isn't a coincidence that I got him on the same day as someone so young was calling out for business, it was the master sweep who told him to go round doing it.'

They argued on, and things came to a head when one shouted, 'Stop making excuses' and it looked like they were going to start hitting one another. A woman, the wife of one of them, came rushing out of the house to put a stop to it, while the other went away.

'I'll teach him to mind his own business' her husband said to her.

'Well he has taken out private prosecutions before' she replied.

Charlotte had had enough. She crept quietly away with Tooty.

She continued to feel very uncomfortable walking up the driveway of the big new house. She continued to feel daunted as she walked past the big front door. She feared very much that someone would come out and ask her what she was doing.

She hurried round to the back. She felt relieved when Gloria asked her if she could do some washing; it made her feel less of an intruder.

The washhouse was in the backyard just across the way from the kitchen door. It was a one-roomed brick house on its own with a very big glass window that looked out on to the back garden. There were apple trees there, a raspberry and gooseberry bush, and there was also plenty of rhubarb growing. Pears were falling on to the ground from a pear tree. There was a tank in the backyard to fill rainwater with, but there was only just about enough. She wondered where the nearest standpipe was, only to find that too was in the backyard.

'I wish I could have a garden like this,' she thought to herself a little later on as she was hanging out the washing there. She also wondered if she could one day grow some potatoes in it, in a place where no one would be able to see her from the house. In fact, because she was too afraid to use their privy in case someone came out and caught her, she had dug a hole there for her and Tooty. It was some way from the standpipe, so she was certain nothing could contaminate the drinking water. Then she had to dig another one somewhere else. She could only use a hole for a short while, yet she would always know where the last one had been from the flowers that always grew there. It made her think that she should try to grow some food there, as it was making the soil so fertile. Later she did so. During all this time she found it a terrible worry that she had to live in such secrecy, yet nothing would make her go back to the life of the city.

On this particular day, after she had just arrived and was hanging out the washing, a young man called across to her, 'Can you do some washing for me?'

'Of course I can.'

It was David, the nephew of Mrs Everett across the way. Their back garden nearly backed on to the Everetts' garden. It turned out she wasn't a complete stranger to him. He had heard a rumour from another servant girl, and then he had seen her in church. He gave her some money for doing it, and said he'd bring some water over to fill up the tank.

Later on that week she popped into Bowdon Church to do a bit of voluntary work, a bit of cleaning. She was thrilled when she was paid for it. Nothing was organised - the churchwarden took the money out of the church collecting box. She later discovered it suited them to have it like this. She was thrilled with it, no rent to pay, nor did she have to pay for her food.

'I can't go on living in secrecy' she said to Gloria. Then she thought she might have a chance to get a break from it. When she saw David across the garden again, he told her a little about himself. His aunt had big plans for him to be a big lawyer one day, to have a firm of his own and to bring up a family, but for now he was happy to be single and live as he was.

He lived and worked in Stockport, funnily enough in Greek Street, just round the corner to the workhouse where Charlotte had been. His aunt was keen that he was involved in the church, and he was keener still. He found it very convenient that he could stay with her sometimes, although she didn't agree with him taking days off from the office and making a bit of extra money by having a client or two in Bowdon.

The penny post had changed everything. Until not long ago, the receiver of the letter had to pay for it, and it was quite expensive. If the recipient didn't have the money on them it was taken away. But now it was the sender who had to pay, and the stamp was the proof of payment. It meant everything to David - the Royal Mail service was wonderful. He said to Charlotte, 'Now I can find out quickly if the firm need me in Stockport.'

His aunt didn't believe it. 'It won't last' she said.

The head of the firm was an old man, a lawyer who should have retired a long time ago, and the offices were in a house with a flat downstairs, three rooms in it and three offices upstairs.

Charlotte saw David a little later. He said to her, 'Can you do something for me? I told my aunt I was mending something in church with you and Tooty there, when really I was with a client in Bowdon.'

'I'll say whatever you like.'

'Good girl.'

She was glad he had something to hide, because she did too. Plenty. She said, 'I can't stay much longer where I am, I shall have to go shortly.'

'Don't do that' he said. ' I like seeing you around.'

She began to feel the excitement she had last felt those years before with Rodney, but this was something very different. A man of his class couldn't have a romance with a servant girl; it would be difficult even to have a fling.

'Can you and Tooty ride a horse?' he said one day.

'We can.'

'I'll hire some. Where do you want to go?'

She wanted to go to Salford, to the Bible Christian Chapel. She had heard so much about it. It was vegetarian. Next Sunday they went to Bowdon Vale, hired a horse each and off they went.

The chapel wasn't far from Manchester Cathedral. The preacher rose to give his sermon, and the text was Genesis 9.3: '*God said that every moving thing that liveth shall be meat for you, even as the green herb I have given you all things but flesh, with the life thereof, shall ye eat.*'

And so had begun his sermon to abstain from meat. He was much influenced by Dr George Cheyne, (1671-1743) the man the Roman Catholic had told Charlotte about some years before. He preached that a vegetarian diet was good for one's health.

He also told the congregation, 'All mildly disposed animals eat vegetables, while the savages of the forest are universally carnivorous.' He finished up by saying, 'Eating meat is unnatural. If God had meant us to eat it; it would have come in edible form, as in ripened fruit.'

After the service she spoke to some other people attending and found one thing out. She wouldn't be able to get any kind of a job there. Too many other people wanted them.

She said how furious it would make her when people would say she cared more about animals than she did for people. Then someone told her something that made them feel quite angry. That was when it was said that it was the hypocrites that went to church. In fact she told her a joke about it.

A man said to the pastor, 'I can't go to church; it's too full of hypocrites.' And the pastor said, 'Not at all, we've still got room for one more.'

She was beginning to realise what a lot of money David had. Where did he get it all from? Did he have to work? Even he didn't know what a lot had come over from France. When she started talking to him about having to go back to Bowdon he said, 'We can go to the flat in Stockport, I'm too tired to ride all the way back there now.'

'But we've got to take the horses back.'

'We'll have them another day, they know me, they know I always pay up.'

He put them into a stable, paying the innkeeper at the same time. She also had another shock. He expected her to travel from Manchester to Stockport by train. Last time she did this she had said, 'Never again!' The trains went so fast. And how right she'd been, more and more people were being killed in them. One newspaper had written, 'Does no one care?' It seemed to be becoming an accepted fact that you can be killed in a train crash.

'I'm not going to go' she told him.

'Stop being so daft!'

'No, it's you that's being daft' she said.

David won and they went by train. Tooty loved it. She had been so used to horses that could not do much more than 10 miles an hour. She was saying the whole of the time as it raced along, 'Speed! Speed! Faster, faster!'

Charlotte was glad at least that she had David with her, for there was another dangerous thing about these trains; sometimes women were attacked in them. In fact there was talk of building railway carriages with a connecting corridor, so that a defenceless female wasn't left alone with anyone. They were also saying they should get some means for a passenger to call for some kind of help, perhaps a chain running the length of the train, if it could be rigged up conveniently. A tug could sound a bell and alert the driver, but then a steam engine is such a noisy thing, would anyone hear?

It was getting quite late and it was beginning to get dark as they arrived in Stockport and started on their way to David's. As they walked past a public house they could hear a commotion starting up inside. Women were shouting, and clearly an argument was breaking out. It was followed by the sounds of scuffles, chairs falling, tables going over and glasses breaking.

Then the door flew open and two women came flying out. The barman had given them an almighty push. 'Sort your differences out somewhere else!' he shouted after them and immediately closed the door. A crowd from inside cheered him on.

'Come on,' said Charlotte, 'There's going to be a punch up!'

The women continued to fight. They rolled about on the ground accusing one another of various things and pulling one another's hair and clothes. One shook her fist at the other while the other, still on the ground shook her own fist back.

'Why don't the men come out and stop them?' She asked David.

'Oh' he said, 'they're street girls. There's always a row going on about something. Most likely one of them's been trying to get another one's business, has strayed on to her pitch.'

'I still say the men should stop it,' she told him. David didn't think so, though clearly he detested it. She didn't think his attitude was very professional for a solicitor.

The building where he worked in Greek Street was very near to the station, and they soon got there. She found it all very interesting; in fact she loved it.

She and Tooty were soon fast asleep on a mattress on the floor downstairs, for they were worn out. David said he had some work to do. The next thing they knew, light was coming in through the window and it was time to get up and go back to Bowdon.

After they had been back a day or two she went to look at the big house the Bible Christian Chapel had been talking about buying and making into a Vegetarian Society. It was called Parkdale. It would be good if she could get a job there and accommodation.

She stood there gazing at it and began to dream. Twice a horse and carriage went by on its way to Dunham Massey; the earth was well trodden down, so clearly it was more than just a lane, but a well-used road. She continued to stand there gazing at the house. She could see clearly over the wall; it was only a low one but the house was so hidden by trees that she could hardly see it.

There was a shed next to this little wood, by the side of the wall, and she had no trouble nipping over and through the trees to it. No one could see her, and it was beginning to get dark.

She peeped inside. It looked as if it hadn't been used for some time, and it was full of hay, as if a horse had been there. She held Tooty's hand and said, 'Not a bad place to doss down in.' There was a big hedge running across the garden, yet through this hedge she could see some stables. They were only yards away from the house.

They were able to creep round to the back of the house. It was in the country, and she could walk through a field that ran alongside it, jump over another wall and have a good look at the back. She stood halfway up the garden, their long, long back garden, looked up at the veranda, and saw a maid come and draw the curtains. She was starting to get very tired of having no permanent home herself.

Charlotte took a bit of a tour on her way back to Gloria's. She went through the garden of the house next door, which seemed a mile away, though in fact it was only a five-minute walk. She found herself at a mansion called Denzell. She could see a long, wide corridor through the front door, the enormous front door, with lots and lots of rooms leading off it. As she walked on past the house, she could see into some of these big rooms. She was used to houses cramped up all together, back to back, with lots of people having to live in one room, or even in a cellar and with a terrible fear of a fever breaking out. She was beginning to feel less nervous about the secret life she led in hiding; she felt it was these people who should have something to hide, living like this. She also wondered if Tooty was being brought up right, having to accept this.

She continued to help out at Bowdon Church. The church school was on the corner at the top of Richmond Road. It was suggested Tooty should go there, but how could she, she had no permanent address? And was there any point? She could now read and write fluently.

Charlotte and Tooty spent more and more time in the shed at the house called Parkdale, which would one day be the offices of the Vegetarian Society. Sometimes there were hens around, but usually they stayed on the other side of the hedge. Once when she went, a hen could see her coming and was clucking to her chicks to come quickly inside. 'Shush!' Charlotte wanted to say jokingly. 'I'm not supposed to be here'. At other times she could hear the stable boys talking; they were clearly fond of the horses. One day she heard one of them say 'I can't understand it, how some people can eat animals'

It made her optimistic that she was in the right place and that the house would one day be the headquarters of the Vegetarian Society. Another time they were saying that they intended to convert the stables into a house and call it the lodge, but that wouldn't be for a long time, she said.

She found a much quicker way, along the sandy track called Burying Lane. She desperately hoped not to meet any funeral processions on her way, but if she did, she had no need to look. She could soon duck down behind a bush or one of the old fir trees on either side. It went right down to The Narrows, a path people would take when making their way up to Bowdon from The Downs, and in fact, much later, the end of Burying Lane was made into a completely separate road called Bowdon Road.

But for now it was one long, sandy track, and just before it came to the part called The Narrows, another path led off it, known as Turf Lane. This led to Dunham Road where the big house and stables were, and where she dreamed the Vegetarian Society would be based one day. It was a path of turfy soil, damp and springy, also later made into a wide road, which would be called St Margaret's Road, for in 1858 they built St Margaret's Church, just opposite on the Dunham Road.

Charlotte would go along Turf Lane to the shed, sometimes taking a picnic basket with her, and even some blankets. Gloria had got these for her off Samuel's bed, as Samuel was now away at university. It wasn't so much that she felt hidden away lying in the hay inside the shed; it made her feel safer. She felt she could escape more easily. If anyone came out, she and Tooty would soon be able to run through the little wood and nip over that wall into the Dunham Road.

She also discovered something else; the building across the way wasn't a washhouse as she had thought, but the place where they kept the coach, on the other side of the garden. She realised this as she lay dozing late one evening. It was just beginning to go dark when she heard a horse and carriage coming in through the gate. It seemed very close, and she got ready to run. Then it stopped for a few seconds. She thought they were going to come inside and catch her.

She crept out to peep between the trees. She could see clearly. There was a lady getting out of a carriage and a man helping her down. They went round to the back of the house. This somehow made her feel safe. She had never seen them near the front door, and in any case she would still be behind the hedge and next to the wall. She wasn't going to be discovered.

Yet as time went by she accepted it less and less. She told David, 'If the lady of the house comes out and says anything to me, I'll call her a rich git, and if the butler comes out I'll tell him I'm not having it. I'll say, 'Get the police, they'll have to take me away and lock me up in a police cell to stop me coming back and I'll say I'm going to see if I can get a story in the newspapers about a poor, poor, servant woman who has nothing and a rich woman who has everything!"

She was beginning to rebel. David said he'd speak to his aunt about it. That was followed by a nice surprise. He had already discussed one thing with her; Tooty should be going to school. Now she could. They could use their address.

'I'm not going to school, I'm not going to school!' said Tooty.

'You are!'

'Why have I got to go to school?'

'Because I say so, and that's a good enough reason.'

Tooty did not accept any of this 'nonsense' that education was important, but realising that all grown-ups agreed upon it, she knew she would have to go.

'You don't know how lucky you are' said Charlotte.

'Oh, boring old mother!'

'It's very kind of people to donate money to it.'

'Boring old donors!'

Now they had to spend more time in one place. Tooty had to be up by a certain time, washed and breakfasted and out of the house. No more going to the shed. They were back to being permanently in the cellar.

There was one thing Charlotte was very decided upon; she was going to stay in Bowdon. She was going to save herself and Tooty from the city. She was hearing more horrifying stories about the poverty there and how the conditions were getting worse. Country life was changing and more country folk were flocking to the cities, and this meant the towns needed more food. They could get it there, thanks to modern transport, but prices were high. Sometimes there would be a series of bad harvests, and disease killed many sheep and cattle. They would talk about such problems as keeping the hay dry during the winter to stop it rotting, so the farm animals could have it, and storing vegetables for the same reason. Oh, how Charlotte wished people would keep to a plant-based diet and not waste so much of it by filtering it first through an animal! It also used up so much land.

Life had been getting harder for the farm labourers, as machinery took over their work for them. If they lost their jobs, it often meant they also lost their homes. They would be forced to come into the town, only to find row upon row of cottages built back to back, all very badly drained. On top of this the conditions in which they had to work were unbelievable, and factory accidents were horrendous. Charlotte thought she'd heard the lot, and she told Tooty all about it as she climbed the hill with her on her way to school.

'If we have to beg we'll beg in Bowdon' she told her.

Then Charlotte got another shock. She hadn't heard the lot after all. A girl working at Hollins Mill, Marple, had been so badly treated that she had died. She wondered what else she might have to stand up to, for she had never imagined anything as bad as that. It was only a horse ride from where she'd lived in Stockport.

'Surely that's murder?' she thought. How she'd wished she'd known this was coming, been able to hide the girl away somewhere safe. It also worried her that one of the girls might be someone she'd known at St Thomas' Church in Stockport. It wasn't, in fact.

She also worried a lot about Tooty. She must never get into the hands of such cruel employers, and she prayed that she would always be there to make sure of it.

Every year during the 1850s there had been an outbreak of typhus and dysentery in Altrincham, and many people had died. Whatever would Tooty do without her? Every year health officials would be tearing their hair about it, getting more and more frustrated as they continued to fail. Charlotte kept out of Altrincham and Tooty was forbidden to go, yet sometimes it was someone in Bowdon that died.

Hollins Mill had been built as a powered spinning mill in 1836 by Charles Walmsley, who had been a Stockport lad and married a Betty Braddock. He bought Hollins Estate in the centre of Marple to build a mansion for himself, his wife and his growing family (they are now council offices in Memorial Park).

Walmsley knew nothing of cotton mills or spinning, but that didn't stop him starting up the business. The mill was facing Hollins Lane with a row of cottages at the far end for the apprentices, which were knocked down at the end of the 1800s. Walmsley would help orphans by giving them work. Using child labour wasn't unusual then. By doing this he was also keeping down the cost of labour for himself, but he was not a bad employer; some were cruel, even wicked. Walmsley would provide the orphans with clothes to wear to church on Sundays, and he would go with them there.

However, by 1852 Charles Walmsley was dead and his two sons, John and William had taken over. How different they were from their parents! They brought in a lot more labour, and no one knew for sure where it was from. They came from everywhere, the workhouse, the highway and from all over the country as far as Devon and Kent. Some of them were very badly behaved.

Some workers came from the Isle of Skye in Scotland. There was a potato famine there, not unlike the terrible one in Ireland. The crops failed, and as potatoes were such a big part of the workers' diet they were being left to starve. Skye was on its knees to the English for help.

A man called McKenzie offered to step in, telling parents that he knew of a place called Marple where there was a nice little mill. He said that if their teenage daughters went to work here they would be educated. He made promises that they would learn to speak English and to read and write, and that they would also learn to sew and knit. He said that in return they would be expected to work four hours a day and would be given three shillings a week. He said that if the girls didn't like it, their kind employers would pay their fare home.

The parents didn't feel so confident. England was a far away country and Skye was just a small island off Scotland. Also, Gaelic was the only language they could speak. Yet they were persuaded.

Eleven girls went. They left Skye in May 1852 and travelled by steam boat to Glasgow. No one was with them, though they had been promised there would be, but they were met in Glasgow by a Donald Ross, who found them clothes, food and a bed for the night. The next day they continued their journey, probably by train to Manchester.

The clothes Mr Ross provided had been donated to him to give to the poor, although he sold most of them for profit. At Manchester the girls were sent on to Marple, maybe by goods wagon, as Marple Station didn't open for another 13 years. Mr Ross promised he'd come and join them, but they never saw him again.

Then the nightmare at Hollins Mill began. No agreement was kept. They were working from six in the morning until six at night and paid only a few pennies. They were given very little food, and only saw books on Monday evenings when a schoolmaster would read to them.

It was not unusual for there to be beatings in a mill, but at Hollins Mill they were frequent. A large, rubber strap was used. One of the reasons the workers were punished was for wasting cotton, which was hard to avoid with spinning. Children would be employed to deal with it. They didn't have to be paid so much, so it made sense to have them. They would have to crawl beneath the machinery (while it was still operating) to gather up the loose cotton. Those who did this were known as scavengers. Many died getting caught up in the machinery, and those that didn't had permanent stoops or were crippled by the prolonged crouching that the job entailed.

The English girls would put any wasted cotton on the Scots girls' pile, so they would get the beatings. They could barely understand English and they spoke it even less. All the girls lived in fear of their lives. When one of them was overheard saying she would rather cut her throat than stay there, a supervisor picked up a knife and pretended to offer to do it for her.

Although some did write letters to their families in Skye, the bosses managed to stop the letters getting out. When their families heard nothing, they began to ask questions. One girl, a Marion Robertson, aged 18, did manage to get a letter out and her family received it, but when this got back to Marple she was beaten about so hard around the head that she died. Her 17-year-old sister Catherine was working at the same mill.

Meanwhile her parents, having received her letter and not knowing what had happened, went to the minister, Mr John Forthes, and asked him to write to Hollins Mill saying their daughters must be sent straight back. Forthes wrote twice, but both letters were returned. It wasn't until they threatened to petition the Secretary of

State for the Home Department that they got an answer. They were told anyone could come for Catherine Robertson and two other girls whose parents were about to leave for Australia. These parents too had been trying for some time to get their daughters back.

Alexander Robertson, their brother, who could speak English, went straight away to get Catherine, and was told when he got there by the mill's doctor, that Marion had died of a fever. However, a Scots kitchenmaid told him what had really happened.

Ten other girls also went back, but two of them, Mary and Ann McKinnock, were too late to see their parents, because they had left for Australia.

The promise to pay the girls' fares back to Skye was broken. Their best clothes and shoes were taken off them, and so was any money they'd saved up. But Betty Walmsley, the widow of the original owner, showed some kindness. She gave Catherine Robertson a black dress and black bonnet to go home in. However Catherine was so weak and undernourished that she died soon after her return to Skye.

Both girls and boys would constantly be running away from the mill, but they would always be caught, brought back and punished. Beating children was accepted by a lot of people. In 1851 eight children from Hollins Mill were sharing an unmarked grave at All Saints Church in Marple.

Greedy, respected agents could traffic in human misery. In 1856 two boys got three months' hard labour in Knutsford just for running away and breaking the terms of their indentures. Yet it wasn't considered the worst place of all. Ancoats in Manchester was the real death black spot.

In 1855, although the mill was failing, things started to get better for the workers and it kept changing hands. Little did Charlotte know how much better it would eventually get, and that it wouldn't be closed down for another hundred years, in 1954. It was finally demolished in 1957.

Charlotte would walk sadly around Bowdon, thinking about it all and determined to stay there. She found she could do some work for Bowdon Church, and they would continue to give her some money out of the collecting box. She didn't always attend there. David would sometimes give her money if she asked for it.

She would get the horse-drawn bus early in the morning, in the square just outside the church and the Griffin, and catch a barge to Salford. It would take her an hour to get there. Here she could attend the Vegetarian Bible Christian Chapel. She got to know some of the people there quite well. But she always had to come back to Bowdon.

The curate's wife at Bowdon Church, Mrs Lomax, had a daughter called Miriam, the same age as Tooty, and the two girls would play together sometimes. This shocked many people and was greatly looked down upon. A servant girl's daughter playing with someone of a different class - tut tut, whatever is the world coming to!

But Mrs Lomax had her reasons and knew she would be able to give quotes from the Bible about it should she be challenged. Charlotte would meanwhile be doing some cleaning in the church, and would then have lunch outside afterwards. Monica, who was working for Mrs Lomax, would bring it out to her, and she and Tooty would sit on a bench in the churchyard eating it. They both loved it.

Mrs Lomax, the curate's wife, had been brought up a snob and believed she was superior. She looked down on servant girls, yet she could see how things might change in the future. She also knew that the Methodists and Baptists were opening up more, and attracting quite a few new people including many of the middle classes; many of the workers hadn't the time to go.

In 1851 a survey was carried out in England and Wales of people who went to church on Sunday. Church leaders were shocked at some of the results. They wanted reforms in their churches, while Mrs Lomax wanted greater equality.

After Tooty's first day at school they went round to Mrs Everett's. David, now back in Stockport, told them to do so. Mrs Everett already had two girls from the workhouse working for her. When Charlotte knocked on the front door one of them came and let them in. They waited in the front room and Mrs Everett soon appeared.

'What did you learn about today?' she asked in a jovial manner, more to make conversation than out of genuine interest. 'Did you do a lot of singing?'

'No, we learned about the French Revolution.'

'Really! What did they tell you about that?'

'In France a lot of rich people didn't care that poor people were starving, so the poor people cut all their heads off.'

'*Really!*'

Then Tooty went into it a little. 'Miss Jones said that if you worked in a kitchen for some very rich people, then you could help yourself to a little bit of this, and a little bit of that, but that's stealing.'

Mrs Everett was amused at such honesty but didn't want to say anything that would encourage her to steal, especially as she had her mother with her. Charlotte felt embarrassed and said, 'Doesn't it show she's never been hungry?'

Mrs Everett, speaking slowly and thoughtfully, said to her, 'You know I think Miss Jones is right. I think you would, if you were working in a kitchen for some very rich people and dying of starvation. You would help yourself to a little bit of this and a little bit of that.'

'I wouldn't.'

Charlotte and Mrs Everett decided to leave it at that. They smiled together about it. They were both certain there was no danger there, Tooty wouldn't starve. Charlotte thought about the blankets she had slept under that had been taken off Samuel's bed.

As they were leaving and were standing in the hall, a servant girl

66

came out and invited them into the kitchen. While they were having a chat she got out some cake,

'Don't say we've had this' she said. 'We're only supposed to have it if some is left over after the guests have left. They're having it tonight.'

They all cut a bit and enjoyed it, especially Tooty. It was a long time since she'd had her dinner. She had completely forgotten all that she'd said about not stealing. Charlotte said to her afterwards, 'You are not to take things if people are seriously upset about it, or if it really is behind their back.' She was well aware that in some cases where a person says 'Everyone steals' it merely means that they do.

Chapter Five

QUEENIE

Across the road from the school was a baker's shop. The baker was an old man called Mr Ross, and he didn't open the shop very often. He rented a couple of rooms, one of them very small, from a Miss Smith who occupied the rest of the house with her old aunt.

Miss Smith was very thin, aged about 35, with hair down to her neck, dark and scraggy. If she had looked after herself she could have been quite pretty. She was always complaining. She would shout at the children playing at playtime, saying they were noisy, and would go on about her old aunt. She would use her as an excuse for telling them to be quiet, shouting almost hysterically 'Now I've got an old aunt to look after!'

One day one of the mothers lost patience and shouted back at her, 'What's the problem, weren't you ever a child yourself?' But this only made her rattle more, and the children loved it. Miss Smith was very queenly in her manner, so the children nick named her Queenie.

Tooty found it wonderful that she could play in the school playground after everyone had gone home or at weekends. She would play with Miriam, the curate's daughter, and Oliver, the caretaker's little boy, who lived with his parents, next to the police station, in one of the little thatched cottages opposite the church. When all was quiet they would shout 'Queenie!' across the road to Miss Smith. 'Where's the Queen, is Her Majesty coming out today?' they would call, trying to get her to look out of the window. Then when she did so they would cock a snoop at her, sometimes putting their fingers to their ears instead of their noses. Miriam and Oliver would do this, with Tooty keeping guard to make certain no parents were coming round the corner.

They had to make certain that the headmaster of the school wasn't there, as he had a big house in the playground. Most of all they had to be careful because Miss Smith had sometimes been round to Mr and Mrs Lomax's to complain, and although she would rant on inarticulately and a lot of the allegations were wildly untrue, even physically impossible at times, Mr and Mrs Lomax did know that children can be dreadful, in a case like Miss Smith's they will stir it up and where there's smoke there's usually fire.

'Any truth in this?' they would ask Miriam, looking very serious. Miriam denied it, knowing what trouble there would be if they found out about this latest joke.

Then one day, Miriam, Oliver and Tooty knocked on Miss Smith's door and ran away down the alleyway running along the back of the houses in Richmond Hill, five big houses that led off Richmond Road. Miss Smith chased them. They ran into someone's backyard, and found themselves trapped. She banged and banged on the gate, which they had bolted.

'Come out of there, come out of there!' She shouted. Eventually they had to, and then they ran for it again. But this time they didn't get away with it. She wrote to Mr and Mrs Lomax, and now that it was in writing they were able to sort out the truth of the allegations.

There was more trouble when Mrs Lomax showed the letter to Charlotte. Together they both spoke to their daughters very seriously, saying how shocked they were, and they were both stopped from playing in the schoolyard for a while.

Yet it can be surprising how things can turn out. When the old aunt died, knowing something about being bereaved, Charlotte was most sympathetic. This was an example of people thinking it didn't matter that someone was old, when in fact bereavement is terrible at any age. Miss Smith was devastated and completely bewildered.

Then when she developed a bad chest Charlotte and Tooty went to stay there. She now became known as Queenie by everyone, and the name was being used without malice. A lot of people thought it was her real name.

Charlotte worked hard for her and so did Tooty, and she paid quite generously. She was never mean with money. The baker seemed to have gone, and yet, as he did sometimes turn up with a bit of rent and sell a few cakes, they would keep to the hall or the rooms at the back of the house.

The best thing about it was that Charlotte and Tooty could frequently spend the night in the house. They didn't have to worry about not being seen. It was marvellous getting Tooty off to school in the morning. It didn't matter if she was a bit noisy; it wasn't a secret that she was there, and if Queenie complained it wouldn't really matter. It was marvellous being able to just roll out of bed each morning. Washing was so much easier too, which seemed to make having breakfast much better too. Then off to school Tooty would go just across the road.

Charlotte would still see David sometimes in Bowdon Church, though he spent most of his time in Stockport. He was finding his aunt extremely trying. He told Charlotte how eager she was that he should play the piano. He would play in the church hall, which was also the school hall. He couldn't play very well and she wanted him to practise.

One day he said to Charlotte 'I've told my aunt I was helping you out at Miss Smith's and that was why I couldn't go to piano practice.'

She giggled and told him she didn't mind. The second time it happened she said, 'Don't let it happen too often.'

He told her he sometimes wondered if he should ever have taken law, he was finding it all too much. She began to think that perhaps he liked it that she was just a servant girl and wouldn't expect much. She was glad he was not interested in marrying anyone.

Charlotte stayed in the attic at Miss Smith's as much as she could, for indeed the woman was an oddity. At times she feared her. She could imagine her going completely mad and finishing her days in a mental institution, and she didn't want that. Sometimes she would hear her ranting and raving in the room below and go to see what it was all about. She would be shouting at people passing by in the street.

'Can't you pretend to ignore them?' Charlotte asked her. She wondered how much of what she was saying was true. She knew it would most certainly be correct to say her own little girl and the curate's daughter, had once been busy stirring it up by banging on her door and then running away. But she also knew how Miss Smith's mother had said she couldn't do a thing with her. Now she was finding the same.

She tried to get her to understand that she wasn't telling her to ignore it but to pretend to ignore it. She didn't want her to give them a reaction, see they were having success. Yet she also knew how Mrs Lomax had tried to reason with her about various things and failed. For example, she would say 'Don't stand with your hands on your hips when telling people what you want. It makes you look very bossy and it gets people's backs up.'

Mrs Lomax had also tried to reason with her when she had quarrelled with the grocer at the top of Sandy Lane. She had also quarrelled with the people in the little shop next door. Miss Smith found it most inconvenient that she couldn't go in there anymore. Yet she hadn't been forbidden to, it was just that she was too embarrassed to show her face. She had to get someone else to go for her. She would stand by the window waiting for someone to go by.

'Oh please do make amends' Mrs Lomax had said, 'Can't it be a nuisance to have a row with someone!'

CHAPTER FIVE

Sometimes louts coming out of the Stamford Arms or the Griffin would work her up, or 'get her going' as they put it. Charlotte asked her why she couldn't just slip out of the back door. That would have been very easy. She would be able to go down an alleyway and be in West Road in no time at all. Anyone jeering at her would soon get tired of it and go away.

Charlotte pushed some heavy furniture up against the door of her attic room. At least she would have some warning that Miss Smith was coming. She could see herself being attacked in her sleep and there was one thing she did know, she didn't feel it was safe to go on having Tooty living there.

But Tooty was getting big. She was ten years old now and would soon be leaving school. Then she was offered a job as a scullery maid to a cook in a very big house down Green Walk, just across the way from Bowdon Church. Charlotte hoped that Tooty would one day work in a much bigger house and work herself up from being a scullery maid into a house maid and then be a cook herself. She remained very certain that she must never live in a slum.

But for the time being Tooty was quite daunted by it all, especially when she saw all the saucepans on the kitchen shelves. It looked like a hundred to her, although there may have been only a dozen or so.

Charlotte was told she could visit her any time. Tooty, as well as having her own room at the top of the house, had all her food provided , the same food as anyone else in the house, and she would have a small wage. Charlotte was sure they wouldn't be bad to her. The people she worked for went to Bowdon Church, and this somehow made Charlotte feel they had a boss to answer to.

Sometimes if they had a dinner party, Tooty would work until ten o'clock at night, and they would also employ Charlotte in the kitchen for a few hours. One night at about this time Charlotte was walking back home past the churchyard when she saw a sad-looking woman stroll in. It was at the entrance by the side of Stamford Cottage where the curate lived, opposite the Griffin.

Charlotte felt sure the woman must have just lost someone. She was about 35, well dressed, and clearly a lady. Then she recognized her; she had seen her in church. She was Alice Wood from Richmond Road.

Charlotte stood thoughtfully watching her. The woman seemed to be settling down by the side of a grave, yet there was no gravestone there. She slowly approached her. She had no need to ask her anything. Almost crying it out and holding out her hand to her, she said 'My daughter has been stolen!'

'Stolen?' exclaimed Charlotte, realising that she meant body-snatchers had taken her. They would have sold her to a medical school. She looked at the wooden watchman's hut, but the watchman was not there.

'Oh it's poor Bert, he can't be expected to do much, he's old now and he's been ill' said Alice.

Charlotte knew Bert the watchman, and she knew he hadn't been well. She also knew how crafty the body-snatchers were. They'd probably manage to distract him in some way.

'Oh, they have done' said Alice. 'Some boys called across to him, 'Come quickly, a body is being stolen!' and he ran all the way to the other side of the church. Then they kept him talking, saying they had been mistaken, while a body was being taken from the other side of the churchyard.'

'Where is he now?'

'I don't know, sometimes they get someone else to do it instead and sometimes they don't. Nothing seems organized.'

They went into the watch hut together. There was a very comfortable chair and a cupboard for things like sandwiches.

'That's another trick they tried to play on him' said Alice. 'They tried to tell him someone was waiting at the gate for him with some supper, but he didn't fall for that one.'

'An old man shouldn't have fallen for the other trick' said

Charlotte, and then went on to ask what the police had to say about it all.

'Oh they've looked everywhere' she said. 'They gave up some time ago.'

'Still, you will see your daughter again,' said Charlotte. This was Alice's whole point. She believed that because her daughter was no longer buried on consecrated land she was no longer in heaven.

'I can't believe a loving god would do that' said Charlotte. She knew how her own mother had rushed to have her baptized when she was a baby, believing that if she didn't she wouldn't have a place waiting for her in heaven, but Charlotte could never accept that God would damn an innocent child. Her mother had also believed that there was no place for you in heaven unless you were buried in consecrated ground, or next to it.

Later, doubts about this crept upon Charlotte's mother, doubts she told Charlotte about, and she had her suspicions that the Reverend Martin Gilpin wasn't convinced about it either. Although the three of them never got together to discuss it, they each had their own private thoughts. All three suspected that belief like this had originated from someone's desire to have power. All three of them had noticed people doing things to suggest they didn't believe it, but Alice Wood believed it.

'They won't let you be buried in consecrated ground if you commit suicide or murder' she said.

'I can't see that it follows that if someone is taken out of a churchyard then it means the soul has been taken out of heaven.'

'I came here with my husband, my son and daughter in 1849 when the houses were first built in Richmond Road' said Alice. 'Everything was all right until my daughter Rosemary got cholera, and she was dead within two days.'

'My husband died of that.'

They both cried together.

'Well at least you know where he is' said Alice.

'I do indeed' said Charlotte. 'He's buried in a pauper's grave, next to consecrated ground. Even if he wasn't I would still be certain his soul is in heaven.'

If she hadn't believed this she would have done her best to get the land blessed so that it did become consecrated ground. The fact that people didn't was one of the things that suggested to her that they had the same beliefs.

She held out her hand to Alice. 'Mrs Woods, you must come now, it's late' she said. They walked down the hill together, and then as they stood at the gate together she said to her. 'I shall never get over my daughter dying.'

Charlotte called after her as she walked up her path, 'I'll pray for you, and that will be to a god of love.'

When Alice got in she wondered if she would be able to get the land where Charlotte's husband was buried consecrated so that he would have a place in heaven. When Charlotte got in she prayed to God that Alice would have peace of mind and know that wherever her daughter's body was, her soul was in heaven.

* * * * * * * * *

Meanwhile things at Miss Smith's got more stressful, in some ways. Her legs started getting bad, and she found it so difficult to get upstairs that the bed had to be brought down and put into the back room downstairs. At least this made Charlotte feel safer up in the attic, when she could hear her ranting away.

Miss Smith didn't want Charlotte to go, and became more and more dependent on her. Charlotte found it very handy to be able to slip out of the back door, down the alleyway and into West Road to meet David. The passage there was full of bushes and they could hide inside them. It made them feel 19 again.

One day they slipped away to the Downs, where they felt even more hidden away. Yet they worried at the same time about being seen, a gentleman with a servant girl. The walk took Charlotte right back to the day she had first arrived in Bowdon. How strange it had all looked to her then.

Yet people feared the worst. The opening of Bowdon station had caused a stir. Many cottages had been converted into shops, and others had been demolished in order to build more shops. People were asking how long would they still have the meadows. A few extremists were saying that Altrincham would eventually become no more than a noisy town, chock-a-block with horses and carriages. The population was now 4500, and people had said it was bad enough in 1831 when it had risen to 2700. Some very old people remembered the good old days when if you wanted a house you just put one up, to have whatever taste you wanted, but now in 1850 this was considered very careless. People were saying sanitation and clean water had to be considered. Some people said it wouldn't last long.

The Sanitary Committee had a meeting about it in 1849, taking advantage of the Public Health Act of 1848. The problem of overcrowding was bringing it all about. 'Well I'm not shifting,' said Charlotte, realising she was an extra body there.

As she and David came to Wellington Place she saw again the two cottages she had noticed on her first walk up that hill to Bowdon. But this time she didn't turn back. They walked on across a farm that extended to New Street, although it had hardly been built upon and remained nearly all farmland.

Then suddenly they had a shock. They were in a slum. They were in Chapel Walk, later to be called Regent Road, but in the 1850s it was barely more than a narrow passage in which two vehicles could hardly pass one another. It was badly lit and very badly paved. On the corner of Railway Street stood the Woolpack Hotel, with a very low thatched roof, while in Chapel Walk (Regent Road) there were a few cottages and a bakery. The bakery had a room above it, but could only be reached by a flight of steps outside called Jacob's Ladder.

One of the small houses was licensed to sell beer, yet the landlord wasn't willing to serve just anyone. If a man who looked poor handed him a gold piece, he would tell him that he thought his wife needed it more at home.

Just up the path from this beer house was Farthing Lane, and on both sides of this short cul-de-sac were cottages. Chapel Street also led off Chapel Walk; the houses were few and had gardens and roses. Several industries had flourished there at various times, such as bobbin turning and silk turning.

Charlotte was horrified by what she saw, yet she had seen it all before in Stockport. People were throwing excreta on to the road and it was left there to dry in the sun or to be washed away in the rain. Yet there were gardens around Chapel Street with food growing in them. Charlotte thought it a shame that all this human waste wasn't buried and used as manure, but she wondered at the same time if doing this would let it seep through into the wells and water pumps.

The cottages were smoky and damp with ill-fitted windows. There were public pumps, but only one to as many as 150 houses. She noticed a tall young woman leaning up against a wall and asked her what she was doing.

'I came after the potato famine' she answered in a thick Irish accent. She said her name was Doreen Fitzsimons. Charlotte knew there had been a bad famine in Ireland a few years earlier in 1846, yet she wanted to tell her that she would die from disease if she stayed in that part of town much longer.

'Have you thought about getting a job in service?' she asked the woman.

'Would anyone have me?'

'Well, what are you doing now?'

She said she worked at Bowdon Mill at the bottom of Sandy Lane (Stamford Road). It made bobbins for mills in Manchester.

'Where do you get your drinking water from?' she asked her.

'There's a spring with plenty of it on Hale Moss, but I don't like to go there, because it's where they do cock fighting and sometimes horse racing' she said. 'But there's a big well just opposite the Malt Shovels at the bottom of Well Lane.' (Later Well Lane would be called Victoria Street.)

Charlotte already knew about that well. In fact she had once stopped there while on her way to market. It was a big well, and had become a place to meet and gossip. Charlotte never continued up that short hill where the Market Place was. It was just outside the Town Hall, later to be a public house called the Market Tavern and next door to another pub called the Orange Tree. It was on Church Street, the one that led so very soon on to the Dunham Road. Charlotte had heard about the public floggings they had at this market place and she couldn't bear to go anywhere near it. She had no understanding of anyone who could stand and watch, yet she did know that it gave some people a buzz to see such things.

Doreen talked on. She said there was plenty of clean water around where she worked. She could nip over the wall into the garden of Spring Bank, plenty of springs there and no one had ever tried to stop her. She could also walk a few yards to a lane later to be called Spring Road. She spent more time at work than at home. She could fill herself up while she was there.

Charlotte had noticed that several households kept pigs for bacon, thus putting more excreta out on the road and using up more land and food in order to feed them. She pointed this out to Doreen.

'I know' she answered. 'We managed on practically nothing but potatoes in Ireland until the crops failed. We were so healthy and tall.'

'When you finish work, you must come up and see me sometimes, you work at the bottom of Sandy Lane and I live just at the top' said Charlotte 'You should keep away from here as much as you can.'

'I would love to. I lost all my family in the potato famine, and it's so overcrowded where I live now.'

Doreen had moved once in the hope it would get better, from Hope Square to Beggar's Square, both off Chapel Walk. But there was one good thing. Bowdon Downs potatoes still grew on the Downs, and they weren't expensive.

* * * * * * * * *

Most of their walk had been delightful and had made both Charlotte and David want to live in the country, but she was glad to be back in Bowdon. She was up first thing the next morning to get on with her chores.

She hadn't seen Mr Ross, the baker, for some time, so she thought it was about time she made some enquiries. She went to see his daughter that afternoon. All was well, but clearly he would never be coming back. 'I don't explain that to him' said the daughter, 'I let him get on with talking as though he will be back.' It made Charlotte feel sad. The front room seemed lonely without him, but after this they would use it sometimes.

Then Miss Smith began to believe that there were other people living in the house, people who shouldn't be there. It became eerie. Charlotte knew for a fact that no one had been in the house. She looked for things like footprints. Then Miss Smith said someone had got in through a window.

'Did you see him climb through?'

'Oh yes, I saw him.'

Charlotte knew it was physically impossible. The cobwebs were in the same place, unbroken. The window hadn't even been opened. It made her blood run cold. But it made her feel needed. It also made her feel she had more control over things. In many ways, almost as though she was the boss, it was so much better than working for someone rich, but you had to call her 'Madam'.

Miss Smith started saying her legs were bad because a snake had bitten her, though according to the doctors it was varicose veins.

'A snake!' exclaimed Charlotte, 'We would have people round from the Department of Health, and goodness knows what would happen!'

But Miss Smith was insistent. She told the story of what had happened. When Charlotte told David, he said, 'That sounds most Freudian,' explaining to her who Freud was and what the word meant.

Then something happened which made her decide she had had enough. The papers reported that a man had escaped from prison, and Miss Smith took it into her head that he was the man living in her attic.

'But Queenie, how can he be?' said Charlotte. 'I'm up there and I would have seen him!'

'He's in the room opposite you.'

Queenie reported it to the police, who came round and had a look over the place. They tried to give Charlotte some comfort.

'You always find a few eccentric women saying this after an escape, you're doing a great job here, try to take it all in your stride' said the officer.

But after there was another incident, Charlotte could not take it in her stride. She was woken up one morning by banging on the front door. 'What is it?' she anxiously asked, wrapping her dressing gown round her as she answered the front door.

There was an angry young man at the door. 'Do something about that lunatic!' he shouted at her.

'What's she done?'

'Read this.' He put a letter roughly into her hand. It was from Queenie to the man's household. It accused them of harbouring the escaped convict and encouraging him to jump over their back garden wall and into the alleyway, the one that led so quickly into her backyard, so he could get inside her house. The young man lived in Sandy Lane and his back garden did back on to all that.

'You're an educated man, surely you can ignore it?' said Charlotte. 'Clearly she's not right in the head.'

'She needs putting away!'

'Look, if you don't mind I'll be closing this door.'

To her relief, he went away. But the next thing was that Miss Smith was saying a man was watching her from up the conker tree in the school playground, just across the road.

Such a lot of her talk was who was in bed with who, and Charlotte would exclaim, 'Queenie's to mind her own business!'

Later she was talking about two young women who had been saying what a gay night they had had out together. 'They're lesbians!' Miss Smith told Charlotte, and Charlotte, thinking this was just her again, told her they weren't and that it just meant they had been out enjoying themselves. Later David told her differently.

'Homosexuals have to use a different language because of discrimination and because it's against the law' he said. He also told her why it was illegal for men and not for women. When they took the bill to Queen Victoria making it against the law for men and women to have relations with their own sex, she retorted 'Such nonsense, as though a woman would do a thing like that,' and crossed the part about women out. Consequently, women could continue to have a 'gay' time but men couldn't.

Charlotte wondered how Miss Smith knew such a lot for she was correct in being certain she wasn't one herself. She told David, 'One day they'll legalize it, they'll be free to say they're gay, and then the word 'gay' will just be another word for homosexual and won't be used for anything else.'

She wondered how much it mattered that she had delusions of grandeur. She would come out with the most bizarre stories about what she had done. It was like a dream. One was a premonition that a ship going to America was going to sink, and she warned the president of the United States, so he didn't go on it and his life was saved. She said she had been invited over to America and given a heroine's welcome. Yet she had never been to America in all her life.

Another time when there had been a hold-up at Bowdon Post Office, she said that she had joined in the chase with the police down Richmond Road to get the man. He was running off with all the money, but she had physically held him on to the ground while they arrested him.

She also drew a picture and signed herself RA.

Miss Smith continued to stand at the front door shouting at the children in the school playground across the road, complaining that they were noisy. One morning Charlotte was woken up by it, but by the time she got there she had stopped. The bell had gone and the children were going in.

Then Alice Wood walked by.

'How are you?' she asked Charlotte, looking sympathetic and realising she must be having quite a stressful time.

'No, how are you?' said Charlotte, for Alice looked so pale and thin and class barriers were beginning to break down. She wondered if she should invite her in, though it was hardly a place for a lady. It was clean, but far from luxurious. In fact its condition was deteriorating. Then Alice said to her, 'Come round', so she went within the hour.

As they sat and talked Mrs Wood asked her if she wanted to do some work for her some time, but Charlotte knew she simply wanted someone to talk to. They discussed many things and Charlotte told her all that she'd thought about.

'I'm not the only one who thinks there are people in the church, the same as anywhere else, who are there for the power' said Charlotte. 'And I'm not the only one who thinks this is where all this comes from, you must do as you are told, or you won't be buried in consecrated ground, and you won't have a place in heaven. It may be frightening people into the Kingdom of Heaven, but it's also frightening people to let these leaders dictate to us what we must do.'

Yet if only because of the law of averages, Charlotte was certain of it, there was many a church leader in it for the right reason. She was also certain, because of what they had done, that they believed there would always be a place in heaven for anyone like Alice and her daughter.

'The fact they don't make certain all burial land is consecrated shows this' she emphasized.

'That makes sense, but I daren't hope,' said Alice Wood.

'So you're willing to believe that a man who's robbed someone and so has enough money to make certain he will be buried on consecrated ground will go to heaven, but the man that's poor because he's given all his money away to the needy won't be able to go?'

'That does contradict the Bible,' said Alice and gave some quotes out of it, including the verse that says that a rich man trying to get into heaven would be like a camel trying to get through the eye of a needle.

She found Charlotte a good listener. She told her, 'If you knew how dreadful it is, people just go on at me, telling me what I should be doing and how I have got to live with this. They so often interrupt whenever I want to say anything.'

She had a son and husband living with her, but that wasn't who she was talking about. All her family worried about her. They wondered if she was going to fade away completely. They had even considered telling her a lie, should she ever be on her death bed. Maybe they should say they had found her daughter Rosemary, but they realised that this would only make her die happy. Everything else would be too late. The grief would meanwhile have killed her.

Meanwhile things weren't going well for Tooty. There had been a very big row in the household where she worked. 'Whatever she has done I shall have to apologise,' Charlotte had thought. At this particular moment she was not to get the sack. Charlotte felt completely unable to stand up to it.

'You hear so many yarns you don't know which to believe' said Mrs Lomax, who had been called to act as a go-between. Charlotte intended going round to the woman's house on bended knee, but she had no need. The woman came round to her on hers. She didn't want Tooty to leave. Charlotte was certain there was more to it than that, she wasn't telling the whole truth, but she told her everything that concerned her. They shook hands before she left.

That night a brick was thrown through the front window of the baker's shop. Luckily Miss Smith didn't hear it and slept through it all. Charlotte saw who did it; three youths all laughing, jeering and shouting 'Queenie' at the window. Charlotte went running down the stairs and out into the street to catch them, only to see a back view of them fast disappearing down the hill. It had been her savage instinct. Yet it had made them run away faster and laugh more to see her running so fast.

'What a fool I was to think I'd catch them, and how dangerous it would be if I did' she said to herself, and wondered what had come over her. Although it was late at night, she slipped her cloak round herself and went off down the alleyway to see if David was anywhere about. He was sometimes awake late at night doing paperwork, and so it was this night. He soon comforted her. He told her she was not the only one to respond like that and said people did the craziest things in a crisis.

Charlotte had most certainly found out how fast she could run. 'That's another thing people find out in a crisis,' he told her. He worked in the courts, so he had heard it all before. He came back down the alleyway and they went into the kitchen and made some tea. She was glad she had someone to talk things over with, they agreed, she needed a rest, a chance to get away.

'I'm going back to Gloria's' she said. 'I'll live in the cellar and washhouse again for a while.'

Chapter Six

REBECCA AND RUTH

Alice Wood went again that night to the churchyard. It was winter, yet not cold. There was a full moon and she could see quite well. It all made her feel so close to her daughter. It made her feel she was doing something for her, and that she could be some comfort to her.

Then suddenly she jumped. Her heart was in her mouth. She knew there was someone close by, watching her from behind a tombstone.

When she looked up she saw a figure quickly duck down. She wondered if it was a body-snatcher. She began to get up from where she'd been sitting on a cushion on the damp grass. As she slowly crept towards the stone, whoever it was behind it made no attempt to run away.

Alice approached until she was only a foot away. She wondered how she dared, but then she realised that the watcher was only a frightened young girl, aged about 16 and very shabbily dressed. She was still wondering if a body-snatcher had something to do with her – perhaps he had hired her for something.

'What are you doing here?' She asked.

'I came to pray.'

'Rather a strange way to go about it, why not come to church on Sundays?'

'I can't, I'm a Jew,'

'Well I think you would still be welcome' said Alice, yet she could see how she might think it wasn't appropriate.

'They're not going to build a synagogue in Bowdon for a long time' said the girl.

'How can a Christian church do instead?'

It was the first Alice had heard of a synagogue being built nearby and she wondered if the girl was a Jew at all - she didn't look like one. But as they got into conversation she found the girl knew a lot about the Jewish faith and its traditions.

Then she noticed a large dog sitting behind the girl. She said her name was Rebecca and she was 15 years old. She introduced the dog as Ben. The presence of the dog explained why the girl was not afraid to be in such a place alone. Yet she still wondered whether her mother would worry about her being out at this time.

'She won't worry' said Rebecca. 'We only have one room between us and she's glad to have me gone for a while.'

She told Alice that they lived in a big house and they were the only two servants there. She said there were rules in the house about what time they came and went, so she would jump out of a window. It was the kitchen window at the back of the house and she would always land flat on her feet on the grass there. At times she felt resentful about it. She realised it wasn't her they cared about; it was what people might think. The house had to be kept looking respectable. She felt it should be only her mother who told her what time to come in.

'Yes but now it IS time for you to go home' said Alice, and the two of them and the dog started to walk along Burying Lane. Alice thought about her own daughter, who had died. How wonderful if it all turned out to be a terrible nightmare and she was back again walking by her side.

As they passed the footpath leading to St Margaret's Church,

Rebecca pointed at a spot across the way from it and said, 'A synagogue will be there one day.'

'Oh yes and on what day will that be?' said Alice thinking this was very far fetched. 'Burying Lane hasn't even been made into a road yet.'

In fact Rebecca was still calling it The Firs, because of all the firs along both sides. But Alice did know they intended building another road leading off it, going down to Altrincham, and calling it Cavendish Road, after Lady Cavendish. She wasn't certain which way they should be going.

'Come along this path' Said Rebecca. 'It's the way from Altrincham up to Bowdon.'

'In that case they should call it Bowdon Way.'

'Well they probably will do once it's been separated and built into a proper road; they will probably call it Bowdon Road.'

Rebecca said she could read. She talked about a woman in Altrincham who had opened up her house as a sort of a Christian coffee bar and bookshop. You could buy a bite to eat there, sit by the glowing fire and have something to read. Various people had donated books. But the woman took care of the place. She still kept the outside looking like a house, and the inside as much as possible too. She called it Mrs Berry's, though it later got nicknamed 'Angels'. It all made her feel quite nervous at times.

There was dreadful resentment about. People were saying Altrincham wouldn't always remain a lovely place of farms and meadows, but would soon become a noisy town, overcrowded with shops and too much traffic.

Rebecca seemed very knowing in some ways, but not in others. Alice remarked that there should be more schools for girls. 'Oh no!" exclaimed Rebecca, 'I don't want to be made to sit at a boring desk all day, leave me alone to go out and about.'

Alice laughed and pointed to her right. 'They'll build it there and call it Altrincham Girls' Grammar School' she said.

'Oh yes!' Rebecca laughed, 'Next to those trees, the ones they call Cavendish Wood. And they'll put an entrance in the road to be named after Lady Cavendish, Cavendish Road.'

They walked past Bowdon Downs Congregational Church. It had recently been built, in 1846, to serve the growing non-conformist population. Alice didn't like it. She didn't want anything else but Bowdon Church. And yet it was the Bowdon Downs one that had recently been enlarged.

It wasn't long before they came to where she lived, in a short road called Norman's Place. Alice slipped through the trees with her into the garden, giving no thought as to what she would say if anyone came out and asked her what she was doing there. She watched Rebecca slip in through a cellar window and then raced back the way she came and into the road. It made her feel sixteen again.

But she didn't feel sixteen for long as she made her way home along Burying Lane. It was a lonely place for anyone to be in, all those firs on either side for anyone to hide behind, but she was past caring about anything. What would Jack, her husband, say? Bereavement can affect people differently. It can break up a marriage. It hadn't done that yet, but they were beginning to go their separate ways. She hoped no one had stolen another body while she'd been away.

A few days later she thought she saw Rebecca again. This time she was wearing a very pretty and expensive dress. She wondered if she had borrowed it from the wardrobe of the woman she worked for without her knowing - she knew servant girls did sometimes do this. She looked as though she was on her way somewhere to enjoy herself. Another time she saw her larking about with some youths at the bus depot just outside the Griffin, and then realised she was attached to one of them. It looked as if he had come on the horse-drawn bus specially to meet her. This time she was quite shabbily dressed. One thing she always noticed was that she always had her dog Ben with her.

Alice decided to contact her again, so she put a note through her letterbox saying 'Come and see me some time'. As she walked down the path away from the house she passed a woman who she felt certain was Rebecca's mother. She was young, in her early thirties, and most certainly looked very Jewish.

Rebecca came to see her immediately, told her that she couldn't have chosen a better time and asked if she could stay a while.

'I can't just take you on like that' said Alice. They sat down to chat. Rebecca told her how she'd read a lot about a very good prophet called Jesus. She said it was fantastic to know that the Son of God was so near to her and her Saviour. 'He died for me' she said, then talked on about the resurrection.

'How long have you been a Christian?' Alice asked.

Rebecca gasped in horror. 'Oh I'm not a Christian! I'm a Jew' she said.

Alice didn't tell her that if she accepted Jesus as Christ, son of God, her Saviour, then she must be a Christian. She wondered what her mother would say. She knew that sometimes a convert can be considered a traitor by the Jews and that families might even disown them.

But Ruth, Rebecca's mother, had nothing to worry about. She had a secret to take to the grave; Rebecca wasn't really her name. She was no Jew. She wasn't even her daughter.

* * * * * * * * * *

Would she ever forget? How could she! That river, what the newspapers had said. How wrong they had got it, but at least 'Rebecca' would never know, poor, poor Rebecca. And yet she had survived it all.

At the time Ruth had only been a kid herself. She couldn't manage. Her parents had come over as immigrants and she had been born shortly after. She had always been brought up to stand solidly by her faith.

Then both her parents died within a month of one another and she was left with a babe in arms. She was devastated. They hadn't been pleased when they first realised that Rebecca was on the way, but they had welcomed her into the family just the same. And they had managed at least to get hold of some papers to say that Ruth was a widow. They were forged, but they did mean she wouldn't be called a 'fallen woman'.

This enabled her to get a job as a nanny to another 'widow' in a big house who had a baby called Mary. For a while all went well, yet they were no normal family. There was no natural love between them, and Ruth was soon to discover that Jeanie was no widow. Like herself, she was a fallen woman.

They plodded on. The house was big and cold, but what Ruth objected to most was the interfering. They wouldn't leave her alone to bring up her own child in the way she thought best. In fact they were accusing her the whole time of neglect. They still didn't know that she was not a widow. They even started implying at times it had been her fault that her 'husband' had died.

Ruth wondered how they had the nerve to tell her how she should be bringing up her own child when they were such bad parents and grandparents themselves. The niggling would go on. 'She looks pale, she looks thin, you should be doing this, you should be doing that!' They would say anything as long as it was criticism. At times it even worried her that they might report her to some authority. Everything was getting unbearable.

November the first. What a dreadful day to remember. It was cold and Ruth had had no rest from it at all. But this time it looked as if they might be right - her child did have a cough and it was getting worse. If it wasn't better by the morning then she would take her to see a doctor.

But next morning, the child was dead. Ruth was heartbroken. For once she should have done what they had said. For once it had been wrong to ignore them.

She picked up the baby and ran out of the house. She ran and ran and ran until she came to a Jewish cemetery, and here she buried the tiny child behind a bush. She prayed for it. Then she went back to the house, afraid to tell them what had happened in case they reported her for some kind of a crime of neglect

So Ruth told a big lie. 'I decided to take your advice' she said. 'I have handed her over to safe hands.'

'Glad you've decided to be sensible' was the only comment they ever made. They didn't know that all her grieving was because the baby was dead.

She still had Mary to look after and she did so with more love every day, yet she would never take the place of her own child. The rest of them continued to show no feeling.

Then Jeanie got involved with a man called Bill. It amazed Ruth that she seemed to care for him more than for her own child. It astonished her that a man would want a woman who put him above her child. Then Bill asked Jeanie to go to London with him. She wanted to go and in any case her parents had told her to get out. 'And take that brat with you' they had said. But Bill told her, 'And don't bring that brat with you.' She panicked, fearing he would go without her. So she asked Ruth to come to her rescue.

'Will you go into lodgings and take her with you?' said Jeanie. 'I'll pay for everything.' Ruth jumped at this opportunity. Jeanie made one condition. 'No one is to know that I didn't take Mary with me' she said. 'I'll tell you why when I get back.'

Ruth was willing to agree to anything. She said she would tell people the baby was hers. She couldn't bear to think of Mary being so unloved in a big city like London.

She often heard from Jeanie, although she got the impression it was simply because she wanted to stay with Bill and make certain there was no chance she'd have to come back to look after Mary. It amazed Ruth how she would complain about him and say she was going to leave him, yet she never did. After one big bust up she did go to Croydon for a short while.

She wrote to Jeanie to say 'It's definitely over between us,' but then she went back to him the next day. He was knocking her about and she had bruises, but she wouldn't leave him. Ruth was writing to her encouraging her to stay, and while clinging to Mary she would say, 'Bill will change.' She knew he wouldn't, but she thought that if she said this it would stop her coming back. She felt that if Jeanie did say she was going to do so she would run, taking Mary with her.

She wrote to Ruth describing the river Thames. The stench! People didn't bother to put sewage into the sewers or where it was supposed to go, everything just went into the river. The river traffic discharged its own rubbish and if anyone wanted to get rid of anything, legal or otherwise, they just chucked it into the river. Bodies, not always animals, frequently turned up there. Murderers would slip their victims into it at night. Suicides would fling themselves off bridges.

When winter came, she wrote about the fog. 'It's dirty yellowy grey' she said. 'It attacks you from all sides, creeping into your throat and nostrils. It gets into your hair, your skin, your clothes, and you can't see your hand in front of you. It's still there with you after you have closed the front door.' But she also talked as though it was something she had to live with. She never mentioned coming home.

Then all the letters stopped. Ruth hoped this was because she had forgotten about Mary, yet she was worried about money. She did still have some hidden away inside a drawer, but it was fast running out.

Then one day she met someone she knew in the park and he stopped to talk to her.

'Dreadful what's happened, isn't it?' he said.

'What's that?' asked Ruth.

'Well that young man of Jeanie's getting killed in a fight and Jeanie going off and drowning herself.'

'No! No!' cried Ruth. She wondered if Jeanie had meant to do it or it had been an accident. Maybe she had had a row with Bill and then had been walking aimlessly about, very upset, in order to walk it off. Perhaps she knew nothing of the fight - that may have happened afterwards.

Ruth was suspicious. Jeanie had once said in a letter how dangerous all the fog was. She said she couldn't see where she was going and one of these days she could see herself in the middle of the road being hit by a horse and carriage.

She had left Mary at home with the landlady, so she went racing round to Jeanie's parents, Mr and Mrs Simcock. They weren't pleased to see her, but they did let her in. They talked of nothing else but how selfish Jeanie had always been, they seemed to show no sorrow that she was dead. 'God knows what she's done with the baby' said Mr Simcock.

'Selfish creature could have left her anywhere' said Mrs Simcock.

Ruth froze. They were not to know that she had Mary. They would demand to have her, and it would not be for the child's sake. Even if she was still around to look after her, it would be very conditional. It would mean she was in their power. They would make threats to sack her the whole time. Perhaps they really would sack her, and she would never see Mary again. No, no one was to know.

She went rushing round to some old friends of her parents, a middle-aged Jewish couple, Mr and Mrs Friedman. She was lucky to catch them as they were leaving very shortly to settle in France. They told her she could stay for a couple of days, and she went to get Mary. She let them make the assumption that she was the child's nanny.

She was exhausted and slept like a log, while Mary slept soundly by her side in her cot. When she went down to breakfast early the next morning, Mr and Mrs Friedman looked very serious. He had gone out early to get a paper.

'I'm afraid the news is bad' they told her, 'The baby's body has been found.'

Ruth looked wide eyed. She knew she couldn't have been. Mary was asleep upstairs in her cot.

'They are wondering if it was losing the child that made Jeanie drown herself and not Bill getting killed' Mr Friedman went on.

Ruth continued to freeze. 'Keep quiet, keep quiet!' she told herself. 'No one knows.'

She kept to her room after that, wanting to say as little as possible. She clung to Mary, knowing that whoever the poor, wretched soul was who had been found it wasn't her. London was a big city - thousands of children died or were found abandoned. How could they have thought this child was Jeanie's?

But they did. The coroner's court confirmed it. Ruth cried tears of bewilderment. Her own child had never had a death certificate, and only Ruth knew she was dead. Jeanie's child did have a death certificate, and only she knew she was alive.

She changed Mary's name to Rebecca, and wondered who would know. Not many people knew her as Mary. Then she had to move on. She ran out of money and the landlady told her to go, so she went into the workhouse. At least it meant she could keep the baby and everyone would know her as Rebecca. She brought her up as her own.

* * * * * * * * * * * * *

Alice Wood had a lovely bath in her tub that night. She had it upstairs in the bedroom, her husband Jack bringing up buckets of water he had heated for her. The fire was burning brightly and everything was lovely and warm.

She knew it was time to get more help in the house, but she enjoyed the privacy of being with just her family. She was happy with the help she got from Elaine, who would come in four days a week to help out, but now Elaine was talking about leaving.

As Jack stood by the window looking out he thought he saw someone come in through the gate and hide behind a bush just by the side of it. He wasn't very concerned. He was used to frivolous activities at this time of night. Maybe it was a woman hiding from a man after a lover's tiff, or someone who had had too much to drink and didn't want anyone to see him. Then he decided it was just a trick of the light and no one was there.

Alice wished she could lie there soaking for ever. She thought things over, how things had turned out. She felt she might be able to sort quite a bit out in her mind if she could always remain so relaxed.

Suddenly there was a ferocious banging on the front door.

'Who is it?' Jack shouted out. He was very alarmed, and most certainly wasn't going to open the door to someone banging like that. Peter, their son, came out of his bedroom. Alice stood at the top of the stairs with a towel wrapped round her and called downstairs, 'What is it you want?' Then they heard a dog barking, and knew it was Rebecca. Her gentle voice could be heard saying, 'Please let me in, I only have Ben with me.'

Once in the hall she came bursting out with it. 'They're stealing a body out of the churchyard!' Jack began to rush out of the house, but Rebecca stopped him.

'I've raised the alarm' said Rebecca. 'Everybody knows about it. The curate, the vicar, and the whole of the Griffin went rushing across.'

Alice came downstairs in her nightclothes. When they looked out of the window they saw two police officers coming up the path. It was

Rebecca they had come to see. She stood in the hall as she told them all about it.

'I had a row with my mother tonight so I came out' she said. 'I went into the churchyard to pray, and then I could hear people talking. They didn't know I was there. It sounded very businesslike, so I wasn't suspicious, I thought they were from the church. Then suddenly I realised I was catching body-snatchers red handed.'

'You were.'

'Oh, have you got them?'

'No, but you managed to stop a body being taken.'

They left, and it went unsaid that Rebecca could spend the night there. Alice now knew it didn't worry her mother how much she was wandering around at night. Then they saw the curate and the vicar walking towards the house.

'Rebecca' they said after they had settled themselves down in the front room. 'You have done a marvellous job. But you must never again be in the churchyard at that time of night.'

She told them how safe she knew she was because she had God with her and a friend in his only Son, Jesus. They both realised she was a Christian.

'God helps those who help themselves and you should not be in the churchyard at such a time' they both told her. They wanted to say that it wasn't helping anyone, but on this occasion they knew it had in fact helped a lot of people. The body-snatchers had left many clues when they had run away, and the police were hoping to find still more next day in the light.

Rebecca went on, 'I thought one of them was following me, so I hid behind a bush in the garden here just at the gate, but whoever it was went straight past.'

'Rebecca, we are going to get a proper rota up so that there is always someone keeping a watch' said the vicar. 'But that someone is not to be you.'

'I only go there to pray' she said.

'Come to church.'

'Can I share the body and blood of Christ while I'm there?' It was something she had read about. As she talked on they both realised she was very keen to be very close to God, to communicate with him, but she did not know that the word for it was in fact 'communion', nor did she know that it was simply the breaking of the bread and drinking the wine.

'You will have to be baptized first.'

'What's that?'

'You will need godparents.' They both looked straight at Alice.

'Yes I'll be one' said Alice, and she thought about Charlotte. Maybe she would be one too, for there was another thing she had in common with Rebecca - neither of them believed in the killing of animals for food. In fact, that was why Rebecca loved the Christian Book Coffee Shop so much; there was no meat there at all.

Rebecca was baptized Rebecca Mary the next day. It surprised them all when she told them that it was her mother who had first started calling her Mary, and was doing it more and more. Charlotte arrived to be another godmother, and Jack would be godfather. Rebecca was amazed that it could be done so soon. She then prepared for confirmation. Alice laughed, 'I don't know why, it's been confirmed all right that she's a Christian' she said.

There was one thing they all soon realised - Rebecca couldn't read fluently. She would sound like a child learning to read. And she could hardly write. But as they knew she was practising all the time, they decided to leave her to it. She was very busy copying things out for the Christian Bookshop. They were short Bible stories on large pieces of paper. Some people love to draw and some people are very good at it, so there were plenty of pictures to go with it.

As Rebecca progressed, Alice wondered if she should speak to her about how she was going to look after herself in life. She felt that this was something for her mother to do, and couldn't understand why she didn't; Ruth was such a good mother in so many ways.

'Rebecca,' Alice asked her, 'have you thought at all how you are going to keep yourself for the rest of your life?'

'I'm going to stay here and work for you.'

'I might not always be here' she said. Since Elaine had left, Rebecca was spending more and more time working and staying in the house, as well as being with her mother and helping out there. She was adamant that she would never get married. 'Men are all right to lark about with' she would say.

Alice went on to talk about her future.

'When you do write, your handwriting is very neat' she said. 'They say they are going to start giving jobs to women as well as to men who have good handwriting. Please keep on practising.'

But Rebecca found such talk quite boring, and in any case she had invented a much simpler way of doing things. She had found a shorter way to write. A mark on a paper which stood for a word was a lot quicker. It was her secret code. She could write what she liked without anyone being able to read it.

On the day of Rebecca's confirmation Ruth hung about outside Bowdon Church. She saw the bishop arrive in a horse and carriage and draw up outside the vestry. She saw him get out of the carriage and give each of the horses a carrot as he patted them. She slipped into the back of the church and sat at the back, thinking about the real Rebecca who had died. She wanted to have them both, as she looked at Mary in front of her but only she would ever know that this was Mary and not Rebecca.

She was so proud of her. She knew there was a very strong bond between them. She thought of how things had turned out. It had troubled her for years that she was bringing up a gentile as a Jew. She always told her, 'You must marry a Jew.' She knew that a British Jew must not marry outside the faith. She also knew that other Jews would not accept it; it was only accepted if it was passed down on the mother's side, but if she could get it passed down the father's side, no-one would know. But this was a solution she had never thought of.

When planning for Rebecca to marry a Jew, she had been more than happy to get a dress for her to borrow out of the wardrobe. It belonged to the niece who didn't come to the house very often. She wondered how much money they all had, that she could have a dress there hanging up for so long and hardly ever wear it. The only other people living in the house were a middle-aged couple and their grown-up son.

Ruth continued to encourage Rebecca to go out to places where there were a lot of young Jewish men, and Rebecca loved to dance. But she hadn't always gone where she was telling her mother she was going. She knew of other places where she could swing the night away, and there was no one Jewish there at all. She loved the music and enjoyed a drink.

One night she had one too many. But at least this time she had gone to where her mother had told her, and it was a young man called Abraham Goldberg who carried her home. She tried to walk by his side, moaning 'I'll never mix my drinks again' and he hissed at her, 'Keep yer voice down will yer!', for she did not realise how loudly she was talking.

He carried her along Slutch Lane – an appropriate name, as it was covered in sludge. She started calling out, 'I'm not going down here!'

'You'll be right in it upside down if you don't shurrup,' he shouted back. He was beginning to forget to keep his voice down himself, and felt like chucking her in.

'I hate Prince Albert!' she shouted, even louder. He wondered what that had to do with anything, and then he remembered. They had intended making Slutch Lane into a road and calling it Albert Road. He didn't tell her they also intended to make the next lane into a road, and naming it Victoria Road, after Queen Victoria.

Next they had to get across streams. The farmer came out of the cottage to complain about the noise. 'Just a bit of consideration for others,' he called across to them. Ben started to bark. Abraham wondered how the farmer would manage after they'd built a new railway station, Hale Station, for there would be plenty of noise then and it was going to be right next to where he lived.

Eventually Abraham found his way back to Rebecca's home. He dumped her behind a bush in the garden and then legged it all the way into Altrincham. Someone was looking out of the window. He thought they had seen him, but they hadn't. He had nothing to worry about. They had merely heard something, and on seeing nothing had gone back to bed.

Meanwhile Rebecca lay behind a bush sobering up. She suddenly found herself wide awake in broad daylight. The loyal Ben was by her side. Had anyone missed her? But her main concern was the dress she was wearing - no one must find her in that.

Quickly she looked among some trees and was very relieved to find her clothes. She quickly changed, then lowered herself in through the cellar window. To her great surprise it was only six o'clock and no one was up yet.

Meanwhile Abraham had gone back to the party and was jigging away with Mary Jane. He was not always entirely truthful when telling his parents who he would be taking out that night. He had told them it was Ruth Abel, for like all Jews they were very keen that the British Jew didn't 'marry out'.

But Ruth knew very little about any of this as she sat there watching Rebecca getting confirmed. It didn't matter if it was right or wrong what she had planned. A solution had come along she had never thought of - Rebecca had been converted to Christianity.

After this she settled down more at Alice's. Her mother Ruth would come to see her and they would sometimes meet in the Christian Bookshop in Altrincham. When Rebecca talked about the Vegetarian Society and how she hated the killing of animals, Ruth would say there should be a Jewish Vegetarian Society. She had talked about it at the synagogue and there were people there who agreed with her. They may say that animals had to be killed in a certain way if they chose to eat them, but they were free to choose not to eat them at all.

'It's a pity I can't join,' said Charlotte when she heard about it.

'You can, you don't have to be Jewish.'

That surprised her, but when she thought about it anyone could join the vegetarian society she was in, you didn't have to be gentile.

Things turned out well for Rebecca as she spent more time at Alice's, especially as she could help Jack with his office work. She got on very well with her writing, which was beautiful. He got her to write his letters for him, but there was something else she could do which he found handier still. She could take down a letter so quickly with her secret code, that he could dictate one to her if he met her on the stairs and then shortly she'd have it all neatly written out for him to sign. He called it Rebecca's Quickhand. Later a man called Pitman would invent a new kind of shorthand, to be called Pitman's Shorthand.

While staying at Alice's and Jack's there was no more jumping out of windows with Ben to meet boys or to go dancing - they weren't having that - but it didn't bother her. She'd had enough. One day she went to see Abraham Goldberg. He was sitting in the garden with Rachael Abel; they were now married and were settling down well to married life.

Abraham said the wedding had been in Cavendish Woods, and there had not been much more than drinking some wine and promising they would uphold the Jewish religion in their new life together. He had given her a ring and said a special vow in Hebrew. Then the marriage certificate was read out and signed by them both. Next he crushed a glass beneath his feet, a custom in memory of the destruction of the temple, but Rachel said it was to remind people that there would always be misfortune as well as prosperity in married life. No one really knew.

It was all a typical Jewish wedding, nothing fancy. It took place beneath a canopy with flowers on, behind some firs in Burying Lane.

'They'll build a synagogue there one day' said Rebecca.

'And they'll build an office for us Jews along Thorley Lane' said Rachel. 'But it will then be a busy road called Ashley Road. The farmhouse will nearly be next door to it, but it will be offices, and the stack behind it will be knocked down and Hale Library will be built there instead. They'll build a road off Ashley Road nearby, the farmhouse will be on the corner of it and it will be called Leigh Road, after Mr Leigh, the farmer.'

'Which farm are you talking about?' said Abraham.

'Ollerbarrow Farm' said Rebecca. 'They'll knock the whole lot down, build roads and call one of them Ollerbarrow Road after the farm'

'Rubbish' said Abraham. 'No one can tell the future like that.'

'Can we stay friends?' asked Rebecca.

'Of course' Abraham and Rachel assured her.

Chapter Seven

MURDER AND BETRAYAL

Charlotte prepared to settle down again at Gloria's. Then she heard some more about Miss Smith. She had had other live-in helps and turned them out. She could be very funny about accusing people of pinching things. She had once followed a helper all over the house, making certain she didn't take anything. She wouldn't take her eyes off her for a second. Then suddenly she came out with it.

'You've got to go!' she said.

'You can't manage without me. It's all right for me if I go, but it won't be for you' said the help. She pleaded with Miss Smith for her own sake alone, but her employer was adamant. 'No I just can't have you here' she insisted. 'You have pinched everything I ever had.'

That was completely untrue. The woman had taken nothing. But she had to go. And it was as she predicted; Miss Smith couldn't manage without her. In the end they came and put her away. She had caused a very big commotion at the local grocer shop. She had stood in the doorway, refusing to budge, and when the manager had said, 'Shoo, now shoo, or I'll fetch a policeman.' She had stood there with her hands on her hips saying 'Well go on, fetch a policeman. See if I care.'

She was later to find she cared a lot. But on that day the grocer ushered the customers out of the back door and none of the others could get in through the front as she continued to stand there giving out her orders with her hands on her hips.

It had all started when a young girl carrying a pile of parcels was walking past her house and she had rushed out into the street and knocked them all out of her hand. The girl was new to the area and it was a completely unprovoked attack. A man walking past helped her pick them up and tried to calm Queenie down at the same time, but she hit him on the head with her handbag. It was the second time she had done this to him; she had done it once in the churchyard. She got away with it that time.

That night the police came and took her away, though she wasn't gone long. No one knows what happened. One day she turned up back again. Had she escaped? It wouldn't have been difficult. The patients often went outside into the hospital grounds, especially when cricket was being played on the pitch that backed on to it. If they played badly a patient might shout across to them, 'Oy, you should be in here with us!' It was only a joke, but it was during one of these matches that Miss Smith disappeared.

Charlotte was glad that she had left before Miss Smith turned her out. It would have been just dreadful if they had had a row. It might have meant she couldn't go back again, and it was a house where she did at least feel there was some security. Now she started going back for short periods, and Miss Smith was always so glad to see her. She knew she had to take care not to lose Charlotte. She would always give her a bit of money.

Yet Charlotte would frequently eat at Gloria's, and she had a mattress to sleep on in the washhouse. She could easily slip out of the window there, into the back garden, through into another, and out of another gate. No one could see her. It also meant she could slip across to David's if he was there. He told her he would see if he could buy a very small house in Altrincham and let it out to her. She hoped he could.

Both Charlotte and Gloria felt certain that the Carltons knew she was there. If not, however did they think Gloria could manage so well? She was working faster than was physically possible for one person. She would pop back occasionally to the kitchen for something and be able to get it so quickly, because it had been prepared.

Yet Charlotte wasn't going to ask if she could get a job there. She had considered it, she would then feel free to live there, but what if they said no? They might put a stop to it all and she could lose everything. She wasn't going to risk it. 'Oh if only David would get that house he was talking about buying and letting out to me!' she said.

Summer was coming. The blossom on the trees in the gardens in Richmond Road was lovely; branches of it were hanging over into the street. She strolled up the hill to visit Miss Smith, but what was going on? She stopped dead. 'What's Queenie done now?' she exclaimed.

Police were everywhere. Had she run out in the street and attacked someone again? If someone was seriously hurt it was an accident, Queenie would never mean to hurt anyone. Charlotte started running up the hill, and then she paused to say a prayer, 'Oh God forgive me for staying away so long.'

A little out of breath after running, she stood at her gate and asked a police officer what Miss Smith had done.

'Who are you?' he gently asked.

'I am a helper, a live-in helper.'

'I didn't know she had one.'

'I come and go. Look, I do know this, she would never mean to hurt anyone.'

'I'm sure she wouldn't. We know her.'

'Oh thank goodness for that, so she's not in a lot of trouble is she?'

'Madam, I'm afraid the news is bad. She's dead. We're treating it as murder. That's why we're here.'

Charlotte went hysterical. She ran all the way to Tooty's, completely unaware that everyone was looking at her. People were coming out of both public houses, the Stamford Arms and the Griffin. They were all talking about it.

'Oh Tooty, oh Tooty!' she cried as she went rushing into the house in Green Walk, for Tooty was now 13 and big enough to be some sort of a comfort to her mother. 'Queenie's dead, poor, poor Queenie!'

She flung her arms around her daughter and they left the house together. No one asked her any questions. It wasn't until later that she realised the whole house must have heard. They were all upstairs at the time, and looking over the top of the banisters. As Charlotte and Tooty walked past the people standing outside the two pubs, they were all looking at them. They all knew Queenie. She had been quite a character. They walked past Stamford Cottage, the place where the curate lived with his family, and down the alleyway at the side of the church.

The days ahead were dismal. Charlotte sat at the front window where the baker used to be, looking out into the street. The schoolyard was just across the road. She could see the conker tree. How could anything be pretty, how could any sort of life be enjoyed when things like this could happen? She had always hoped that things would get better for Queenie. She had never imagined anything as bad as this.

Oh poor Queenie! How dreadful it must have been to wake up and find there was someone in the room with her, for there was evidence to suggest that they had got her out of bed. Yet the police weren't certain about anything. Her body had been found in the alleyway, just a little way from her back door.

So many times she had said there was someone in her house to be told there wasn't. Did she think no one would believe her this time either? How did they get inside? The intruder seemed to have known his way about.

The baker was interviewed. Clearly it wasn't him. Her brother, who owned the house, was interviewed. He was very much under suspicion and known to be a most unpleasant character, a man who hated women. No one had ever doubted his sanity, but it is not usually the insane that kill.

They also spoke to Charlotte about it. She couldn't help. She'd never heard Queenie mention anything of any men friends. Other people in the village knew more. They knew her history. Did Queenie know the serial killer?

Charlotte went back to stay with Gloria, for she couldn't go on living there, not only because the brother intended taking possession - he had now been cleared - but also because she would never feel safe again.

She was numb. She went down to Bowdon Mill at the bottom of Sandy Lane (Stamford Road) to meet Doreen Fitzsimons coming out. 'I'm afraid they're closing this down' Doreen told her.

'It's not safe in Bowdon any more' said Charlotte. 'There's been another murder and it's at the house where I invited you to, the one I said where it would be safe.'

Doreen pointed at the alleyway behind Spring Bank. 'That's where the two others were found' she said. 'It's not safe here either, but I'll see if you can come and stay with me if I can get some sort of a job in service.'

She did manage to get a job. It was in a big house called Holly Bank, next to the mill. It was only until she could find somewhere else. There were four people living there, Mrs Everett's old pal Margaret Wheetman, Jane Williams, the cook, Mary Smyth, waitress and Ellen Taylor, housemaid. The nephew would sometimes come to stay, and being a doctor he quite agreed that Doreen should be kept away from the slum.

Margaret Wheetman, the head of the household, was now failing in health and sometimes a Jennifer Baraclough, a hospital nurse, would stay in the house. Margaret would spend most of her time upstairs, thus leaving the rest of the house hold to feel free to do what they wanted.

'But there won't be much for you to do, with all those other people working there' said Charlotte.

'There's plenty I can do in the garden, growing food and composting the leaves' said Doreen. She went on to talk about how much cleaner the water was. Now that she was a live-in help at Holly Bank she could get enough from the standpipe there. When she had worked at the mill, she had been able to get water from the springs in Spring Bank, but there was another lane full of springs nearby, later to be called Spring Road. It was much more likely to be clean if it came from a spring and not a well.

'Aren't you afraid, with this killer so near?' said Charlotte. She only went to see Doreen occasionally, and even then she always took David with her.

'Not really, there are plenty of us about, and none of us go out at night.'

'I can't see how you'd dare. I don't think you should be in that garden on your own when there's a killer about who's already dumped two girls in the alleyway just across the way.'

'It's only prostitutes he murders.'

'That's only because they're vulnerable, he can get hold of them more easily' said David.

Doreen did go on working in the garden and orchard, but after a while she started to lose her nerve. She found herself looking over her shoulder more and more. All the women became very nervous. They would all sleep in the same room downstairs at night, and try to arrange it so that one of them was always awake. They wondered how safe Mrs Wheetman felt upstairs, so often on her own. At least the house was well bolted up.

Doreen wondered if she should look for somewhere else to live, and if she would find another home with such good security. But Mrs Wheetman very much didn't want her to go. She gave her a pay rise. She felt there was safety in numbers and wanted to keep someone she could trust. When someone asked her why she didn't get a man to work in the garden, she replied that he might be the serial killer.

The four terraced houses across the way had been built for the workers of Holly Bank, and the men living there frequently worked in the stables. Margaret sometimes suspected one of them.

Then there came another blow. David told Charlotte he was leaving her. He said he was in love with another woman. What a time to choose!

She went to Sunday School the following week with Tooty and sat there for part of the lesson. Another girl, called Henriettta, was also there. She was from one of the cottages in Church Brow just opposite the church. She was very upset because her father had been in an accident. He'd been knocked down some steps at the end of an alleyway that ran beside Bowdon Church, by two men wrestling together. He'd had the misfortune to be going down the steps when one of the men caught up with the other and started a fight. They were both very drunk, but one was much more to blame than the other. Henrietta's father received serious head injuries, yet he was just an innocent passer-by. Her mother was determined to get the man responsible.

The child was full of enthusiasm when talking to the Sunday school teacher about it. 'Mummy says...' she would start, and go on about what her mother would do if ever she got her hands on the man. She was after his blood.

Charlotte thought about what the Bible teaches - love thine

enemy. She wouldn't love him. She doubted also she would ever forgive. She wondered how a Sunday school teacher would deal with this. But the teacher just sat there listening to it all and making no comment. The point was that the man was in no way sorry, it was obvious he had no excuse and would do it again.

Charlotte remembered all those years ago, after the riots in Stockport, when she had spoken to the Reverend Bellair about it all. In that case, although an explanation isn't necessarily an excuse, it made it much more understandable. The rioters had been kept in abject poverty. Why had they been so harshly dealt with? Some of them had even been deported to Australia.

When she got to Gloria's, she found that another woman had been attacked, though this time she had escaped without injury. She had screamed and people had come running out of the nearby farmhouse, next door to where they intended building Hale Station. It was in a short passageway called Bath Place, which someone had made by putting up sheds. It was just off Thorley Lane, the road that led to Ashley, and it frightened people that it was so near to Spring Bank. That was where the other girls had been found.

Now they had a description of him. He was medium build, aged about 35, with red hair, and they had made an arrest. They were holding him in custody. The man had once been one of Queenie's boyfriends. David told her, 'They are only allowed to hold him for so long, and then they have to either charge him or release him.'

That night while sleeping in the cellar she was woken up by banging on the window. It greatly startled her. She hardly dared to look; she was expecting to see that medium-sized man with red hair. But it was David. She let him in through the cellar window, then put the kettle on the fire and made some tea.

'It's not safe for you to be here' he told her.

'But they think they've got him.'

'They've had to let him go.'

David seemed to know something about it. He told her that the man was notorious and had already had one conviction for attacking a woman.

'Come with me to Stockport, I'll employ you in my office until you find somewhere else' he said. 'Bring Tooty with you, I'm worried about you both.'

She went. Although officially she was the cleaner, she was in fact acting as a sort of a secretary, and she could make good use of her beautiful handwriting. He appreciated that. She had a very small room at the back of the house upstairs, which had a staircase leading off it going up into the attic. David had a lot of his things up there too.

She wondered how long this could go on for. His flat was downstairs, and he was living there with his new woman, Ethel.

The workhouse she'd been in was just round the corner. She could see it from the window where she slept, and it brought back dreadful memories. She had always vowed she would never allow Tooty to go back there, but now she wondered. She would rather have that than take her back to a dangerous place like Bowdon.

There was one good thing about it; she was back in the parish of St Thomas's. She could attend the church and meet up with all of her buddies again. Then another very good thing happened. Tooty got a job as a scullery maid in a very big house in Bramhall. Perhaps she'd be promoted to a housemaid, or even one day a cook.

But things didn't stay happy for long. When Charlotte visited Tooty, and was in the kitchen with her, Mrs Thompson, the lady of the house, came in. She was very chilly with Charlotte and asked her who she was. 'You can't just come in whenever you like' she said. Charlotte wanted to say to her, 'Shut yer face you rich git!' But she had Tooty with her, and she had to set an example and remain polite. In any case it was crucial that she didn't get her daughter the sack.

'But madam, I don't come often and my daughter is still very young' she said meekly. 'I do beg you to allow me to visit should ever I have concern.'

'Very well' said Mrs Thompson. 'I hope that won't be too often.' She left the room. Charlotte didn't mind saying to Tooty after, 'I nearly put my foot out to trip her up.'

Next time Mrs Thompson came into the kitchen while Charlotte was there, she asked her 'Will my daughter be allowed to come and visit me on Mother's Day? The church has made that a special day for mothers and servant girls to be able to see one another.'

'Of course she will!' said Mrs Thompson. She was very brisk with her answer, as though it was unreasonable for Charlotte to suggest she might not allow such a thing, but Charlotte had said it intentionally to insult, and she felt she had succeeded.

Charlotte wondered what a woman of that class was doing in the kitchen. Shouldn't it be the butler who spoke to her about such things? Wouldn't he feel she was treading on his toes? And what would the cook have to say about it? In houses like that most kitchens rarely see the lady of the house. She nearly told Tooty, 'I've got half a mind to bang on the window when you leave and cock a snoop at her.'

Then Tooty started finding it all too much. She had been promoted to housemaid, and it was even suggested she would one day be a lady's maid. Mrs Thompson had a daughter called Barbara, who was two months younger than Tooty, and she acted as though she was thoroughly spoilt.

'Is she going to have servants all her life?' she asked her mother resentfully. She objected very much being told what to do by someone younger. Tooty had also began to mind that some people had so much more money, for she was certain she was their equal in every other way.

One day she spilled something on the tablecloth and it didn't wash out completely, although you had to look very closely to be able to see it. Barbara went on about it, and Tooty was disgusted. She called her a 'rich git' and made as if to hit her. Barbara, putting her hands up to defend herself, said, 'Don't you dare hit me!'

When Charlotte heard about it she said 'And don't you dare hit her!' But Tooty remained disgusted. She had seen so much poverty. She knew so much more than Barbara did. Without realising it, in a way she was more educated.

'She's a right spoilt bitch!' she told her mother.

'Perhaps she likes showing her authority.'

Then Tooty confronted Barbara.

'Who do you think you are?' she said.

'I think I am Barbara Jane Thompson, 2 Frances Road' she replied. She knew how to be sarcastic.

Charlotte felt proud that her little girl was not accepting everything she was told as she grew up. But it created a problem. Before this, she had had it all planned. Tooty would spend her life in service, and never go back to the workhouse. This way she would always have a roof over her head.

'It isn't quite true they never do any work' she told her daughter.

'Well it nearly is.'

'It does provide you with somewhere to live, and they have to run a house.'

'No they don't. They have a butler.'

'It's not as simple as that. Things can go wrong which they have to see to.'

'They don't have to get up early every morning, sometimes in freezing cold weather, light fires for someone while that person lies in a warm bed and then have to work for the rest of the day as I have to.'

'You don't work all day.'

'I'm on call, I'm not free to go out, that's work.'

'No it isn't!'

Charlotte's heart sank. She agreed with so much of what Tooty was saying. She put her arm round her, looked straight at her, and said,

'PLEASE, for now, do what your mother tells you. Don't upset them just at the moment. Stay for a while. It might be only for a few months.'

Tooty agreed. Then something horrendous happened - she was arrested for shoplifting. The police were called, but they soon let her go because there was not enough evidence. That wasn't surprising, as she hadn't done it.

But when she got back to the house, she found she'd got the sack. She went with Charlotte for an interview, for a job in service again, everything went well and they told Tooty she could start on Monday. The new place was much nicer than the Thompsons', and they felt they would soon get over what had happened.

But then came the bombshell. Barbara had been spreading it around that Tooty had been sacked for shoplifting, and it got back to her new employers. They told her she couldn't work for them after all.

Charlotte wondered how she'd be able to get a job anywhere with this going around, and most certainly Tooty couldn't get a reference. She was deeply upset, but at least she could keep her in the attic at David's. David was away at the time, and when he came back he said 'I'll soon sort the Thompsons out'.

'How?'

'They'll have to apologise. I'll write and tell them that if they don't, you'll be seeing an expert in slander.'

'But we've got no money!'

'They won't know that. I'll say we're employing Tooty, and woe betide them if they say a firm of solicitors is employing a thief.'

Charlotte was amazed at how quickly this worked. Mrs Thompsons apologised at once, and was very anxious to put it right. She wanted it settled out of court, and offered Tooty her job back.

She went to see Mrs Thompson, and saw her smiling sweetly but nervously out of the window as she watched Charlotte walking up the path. Clearly she was scared stiff. Charlotte smiled back, went inside, and spoke to her gently about other things they didn't like. She thought she would take the opportunity.

'Its not for Barbara to tell Tooty what to do, she's too young, she's even a couple of months younger than her' she said. Mrs Thompson agreed. Charlotte also told her about what poverty they had to suffer, how Rodney's health had failed through it and he had died of cholera, so Tooty had lost her father.

'I have to tell you there are some pretty bad things going on among the aristocrats' said Mrs Thompson. 'I've been saying for a long time that one of these days one of the royal family will die of cholera at Windsor Castle. Nothing would surprise me.'

'Well I can't see that' said Charlotte, 'not Queen Victoria or Prince Albert dying of typhus.'

But it had very recently been confirmed that typhus was carried in water. A Dr Snow had discovered it in 1853. Before that many people had believed it was carried in the air, but Charlotte had always thought differently. No wonder other people were suspicious too. Wells were made dirty by sewage from the local cesspit, and the rivers were even worse.

'Windsor Palace should be seeing to it, and to everywhere else' said Charlotte.

'So Rodney died of cholera?' said Mrs Thompson, and then, looking tearful, 'I lost my husband in a war.' Charlotte wanted to cry with her. She had noticed she had only a brother living with her, and that he was away a lot.

The two sat together for a few seconds, leaving things to go unsaid. Silence can be soothing. They talked a little about it. Mrs Thompson said that when it had first happened his family would all sit round the table together saying nothing. They would pass one another on the stairs and not say a word, yet a message of deep grief was still exchanged between them.

Then they got down to talking about other things. Mrs Thompson started getting on the defensive. She said she did sometimes work.

'I've taken in girls from the workhouse, although there's not been a lot to do' she said.

'I told Tooty that you give her a roof over her head, and there wouldn't be too much to do with all those people working here' said Charlotte. She didn't mention that Tooty had retorted, 'And isn't she lucky to have all that money to have all those people working for her.'

It was agreed that Tooty could have her job back for seven years, and if during this time she wanted to leave, or they wanted her to go, they would give her a lump sum of money. She would have a pay rise and a room to herself. But she would still go on being a scullery maid. She wanted to stay as far away from Barbara as possible.

Charlotte decided to say a little more to Tooty about her ideas that all the rich children had an ideal life.

'I have heard very differently about how they are treated' she said. 'It's true they eat well, don't have to work and have nice clothes, but some of these clothes are very uncomfortable, and some of the children are so strictly brought up you could almost call it cruel. They get hit, sometimes even with a stick, for the least little thing.

'I have seen tiny babies in heavy lace, and toddlers barely able to walk in stiff brocades and heavy satin and lace. Tooty, you were always free to run around and play without all that.'

Tooty pointed an accusing finger at her and said,

'Are you telling me it's better to live in poverty than live like the rich?'

'Yes.'

'You can't believe that, and you can say that again, what you said a while ago. Laws to try to improve working conditions! They may be trying, but no one's noticed, we learned about it at school.'

'Tooty, aren't you glad you didn't go to a horribly strict school? That was because of me. I would have taken you away if it had been.'

Charlotte had also heard how cruel some of the governesses could be, beating a child for doing something as small as getting a sum wrong and then not letting her eat anything for the rest of the day. She knew some of them were made to say long and boring prayers, with no idea what they meant. The idea wasn't that one day they would understand but simply that the discipline was good for them. Some of them were told frightening stories about God's anger.

Charlotte didn't seriously believe that very poor children were better off than the rich ones - she wanted to be rich herself. But she would say at the same time, 'I want to be rich and free from all this.' She would think about it when sleeping in stables.

Charlotte felt terrible pangs of jealousy, knowing David was downstairs with his new woman, but she knew she had no rights over him. He had never made her any promises. In any case, how very difficult it would be for someone as humble as she was to be coupled with anyone like him.

She wished she could be a woman of sin, live with him and have him that way. 'I don't care what the Bible or anyone else says' she thought to herself as she remembered Martin Gilpin's words: 'You may deceive man, but you will never deceive God.'

But David's woman was giving her shock after shock. The first wasn't too bad - she had been arrested for being drunk and disorderly. Charlotte wondered how disorderly? Charlotte herself couldn't take much drink - of course she couldn't, she drank so rarely. Maybe Ethel was the same. Perhaps she'd just been unlucky that one time.

But then she discovered how often it was happening. Ethel was being run in for it night after night, and was known as a regular customer down at the police station. The person who told her lived opposite. Her front door faced the back door of the station, the place where they would bring them in. She and her sister would often sit at the window upstairs watching it all. It was a pantomime.

'David, what are you thinking of!' she said when she heard this.

She'd already had another shock when she had first seen Ethel. She was enormous. Charlotte hadn't known before it was possible to be so fat. She was in for another shock when she heard her speak. She had a voice like a foghorn and sounded as thick as a plank.

'David, what are you up to?' she said. Charlotte felt at a complete loss. She was certain he wasn't in love with this woman. She lost all pangs of jealousy and felt she had no rivalry. When she challenged him about it he said that that wasn't the woman he'd been talking about.

'Oh well,' thought Charlotte 'don't ask no questions and you won't be told no lies.'

When she was doing some secretarial work for him, she set out to find out a bit more about Ethel. She decided to look through some papers in the attic. She felt quite nervous doing it, and she had to remember how she had found everything so she could put it back in the same place. No one was to know she'd done it. She locked the front door before she started, yet she still found herself looking over her shoulder the whole time as though she could hear someone coming up the stairs.

One day she did hear footsteps, and she froze. How could she explain the locked door? She thought it was David coming back unexpectedly. Then someone called out, 'Ethel, is that you?' It was not David's voice.

'No' she called back, and she heard him going away. She stood silently in the room for about five minutes, and when she finally ventured out he had gone. She never found out who he was. Tooty had let him in.

She didn't do another search for some days after this. She then discovered that Ethel did come from a good family, but wherever had she got that dreadful voice from? She also found out her original name had been French, and signs that she had tried to hide it. She wondered if she had anything to do with the French Revolution. Maybe she knew things which were confidential, and this was why David was doing this - a sort of subtle blackmail. Why had he sometimes asked her to tell his aunt he'd been with her when he hadn't? Had he been with this woman? Had he always been entirely truthful with her?

One day when David was away there was a gentle knock on Charlotte's door. When she answered it, Ethel was standing there. She nearly fell inside. Charlotte pushed her roughly out, firmly closing the door, only to hear her knock again. She opened it, got a very big whiff of alcohol and said sarcastically, 'Go away, I don't like the smell of orange juice'.

This time she couldn't close the door, because Ethel had her foot in it. A struggle broke out, and they both tumbled down the stairs. Charlotte immediately got up, but Ethel lay there motionless. She was clearly flat out and very drunk.

'Good riddance for at least one night,' Charlotte shouted at her and went upstairs and slammed the door. The next door neighbour banged on the wall.

At about four in the morning Charlotte was woken up again by Ethel knocking on the door. This time Charlotte opened it and let her in.

'What do you want?' she asked her angrily.

'I want to spend the night up here.'

'Clearly you're an alcoholic.'

'So what?'

'So you're a damn nuisance to everyone!'

It wasn't like her to swear, but she couldn't help it. She realised then that she had to be careful. The woman next door had already banged on the wall once.

Ethel settled down in the armchair and Charlotte got back into bed. 'I'm not prepared to put up with this' she thought to herself 'I'm going back to Bowdon tomorrow.'

Ethel was half mumbling something to herself and half to Charlotte. 'There's a lot more to this than you realise' she said.

'What's that?' Charlotte asked her abruptly. 'There's a lot more to what?'

Ethel continued to mutter incoherently, saying nothing that Charlotte could understand. "Oh, so you're not as daft as you look" said Charlotte. She had heard people say you should be sympathetic with alcoholics, but she wasn't at all sympathetic. She also very much suspected that some of the people that said this did so to sound pious. How easy it is to be pious if you don't have to put up with it yourself. And some of those people could so very quickly find an excuse to back out of having to do anything if ever asked to assist. It would always be done in the name of caring.

She also believed that trying to help alcoholics was encouraging it, or at least that's how it would finish up.

'Once that starts, the day will come when it pays to be an alcoholic,' said one person to her, and already Charlotte knew of someone who had pretended to be an alcoholic when they weren't. She felt certain it was sympathy they wanted and found that their whole attitude was 'Oh poor me.'

'They'll be doing it for the money next,' said Charlotte, when she heard it suggested that they should have some money from the poor box. She found that people who drank didn't care about how much damage they were doing to anyone else. They just thought about themselves.

She had now met a young woman called Catherine Mumford, who

was madly in love with a man called William Booth. He was tall, dark and handsome and she dreamed of him the entire time, saying, 'One day I'll marry him.' It reminded Charlotte of the way she would dream about Rodney.

Catherine and William planned to set up a Christian Mission together and call it the Salvation Army. Catherine did not accept it that it was unthinkable that women should preach, and this caused quite a stir. She believed in equal rights, and was dedicated in many other ways. She did great things for the poor, including getting money from the rich to give to them.

She had a house full of pets, and like Charlotte she was a vegetarian. She had been in the country and couldn't bear to see lame lambs being made to walk. William Booth later became General Booth of the Salvation Army, and many years after that Bramwell Booth, their son, became General Booth in turn.

All three of them were vegetarians, and all three were also dedicated to the problems of drinking. Charlotte didn't have the patience, but Catherine did. She would visit them in their homes, help them make a fresh start and hold cottage meetings for converts.

'They'll go back to drinking,' said Charlotte. But they didn't, not always.

There was another thing both Catherine and Charlotte knew something about; it was something that Charlotte had already told Tooty, how some of the rich treated their children. Catherine told Charlotte that apart from their clothes being very difficult to play in, all playing was discouraged in any case. The wealthy didn't like their children to run, be noisy, or get dirty or untidy. She wanted something doing about it. She especially felt that Sunday shouldn't be a day they dreaded. Yet they were expected to sit quietly reading dull books, and attend church three times a day. Here they would sing, long, boring hymns, listen to endless sermons and say interminable prayers.

Catherine and William talked of changing all this. 'Why should the devil have all the best songs?' said William. He planned with Catherine to get people closer to the Christian faith with tambourines and banging drums.

Charlotte, however, continued to feel unchristian. Next morning she turned Ethel out very early. She stood at the top of the stairs watching her go slowly down, and when she saw her turn round to look back up she said, 'Keep on going or I'll chuck you down them stairs like I did last night!' Immediately after she'd gone she left for Bowdon, leaving a note for David.

When she got to Gloria's, she knocked on the scullery window. Gloria came rushing to the back door to let her in.

'I'm so glad to see you!' she said. 'They're talking about getting another maid and I don't want that. I want to be on my own. Yet I have to admit to it, I can't always manage.'

Charlotte settled down in her usual place in the cellar. Things were now so much more relaxed. Both the Carlton boys had grown up and left home. There was only Mr and Mrs Carlton in the house, and they would go away for days at a time. Gloria would then be on her own. She told Charlotte she could sleep in her room sometimes, the room above the kitchen. 'I can go up to the one in the loft,' she said. 'I like it there.'

When the place was deserted, Charlotte would creep up the two stairs from the lobby into the hall like a mouse coming out of its hole for the first time. It was a place she had never ventured into before. She saw the front door for the first time from the inside; it still looked so big and daunting. Yet as time went by it seemed smaller. She would creep first into the hall and then up the first flight of stairs into Gloria's room above the kitchen.

Things didn't always remain quiet, or at least not when she attended church, mostly still at Bowdon. One day the parson was preaching about equality. A servant girl sitting next to her hissed in her ear, 'I don't know where he gets the nerve for all this!'

As the singing started up another servant girl in the same row said, 'Ask him then, if he believes in equality, why do we have to sit at the back while the gentry sit in the front?'

They hadn't kept their voices down enough. Some youths had come in shortly after the service had began and were being silly and giggly. 'Ask him this,' said one of them, 'why is it that pews for the rich are padded, lined and cushioned while the poor have to sit on stools in the aisle? When we have to pray, the only place we have to kneel is on the damp stone.'

The two servant girls wished they'd never started it. One of them turned round and quietly told him, 'Don't exaggerate.'

Then a posh voice, also from the back, said, 'That's only according to what someone wrote the other day about a church in Ipswich'.

Charlotte wondered how she could possibly argue that one. Maybe only one paper had said it was as bad as this, but there were rent pews in Bowdon Church, and the rich paid yearly to have their own pews. It was only if they didn't turn up (which wasn't unusual) that a servant girl could go and sit in them. If they hadn't arrived by the time the service was about to start, a bell would ring to tell the congregation. If the church was very full the servants had to stand at the back, sit on stools in the aisle and pray on the stone floor.

Lady Dale, though, seemed to have read Charlotte's mind. She said 'They intend to rebuild this church so that there is room for everyone'. One man shouted 'There's someone in here who has asked to be buried under his pew one day'.

'Will you mind your own business!' another rman shouted. But it was found out later to be true.

Lady Dale was sorting out some hymn books and Lady Cavendish was with her, also trying to make tactful comments. There was another reason for them being there. Things had sometimes gone missing from the back, and they didn't always think it was the poor taking them. Some of the books weren't the sort you would expect them to read.

Charlotte felt daunted by it all, yet she plucked up the courage to turn round and meekly say to Lady Dale, 'I think that some of the poor think the parsons are supporting the landowners.'

Lady Cavendish looked thoughtful. She replied, ' I do know that the Baptist and Methodist church are attracting more people. Lady Dale agreed with her.

'Yes, they feel out of place here,' said Charlotte.

Lady Cavendish had been reading up on the subject. She was well aware that it was being widely discussed, and that many church leaders and other campaigners wanted more doing for the poor. For example Lord Shaftesbury wanted reforms for the workers in the factories and mills.

The next Sunday, it was worse. Charlotte sat at the back with Tooty. When the parson came to the bit about Jesus turning water into wine, a man standing behind them called out, 'Better bring 'im in 'ere then!'

Charlotte turned round in anger. 'Just shut it will yer? Just shut it!' she hissed.

It was one of the bellringers. There had been trouble about their drinking. Lady Cavendish, again at the back, came rushing towards Charlotte saying, 'And you are to be quiet too!'

'What, shut my face?' she very meekly asked her, remaining very polite.

'YES!'

The bellringers did look the worse for drink. A man in the congregation commented, 'I thought the bells sounded a little out of tune as I was walking up the hill.' The parson must have heard that, even though he was some way away, yet he continued with his sermon as though nothing had happened. Then he forgot all about what he had prepared, and started to preach about the devil instead.

'He's happy in his work when people are making themselves look silly' he said. This was followed by complete hush as everyone listened.

Charlotte missed Tooty, all those miles away in Bramhall. She would walk to see her, but it was a long way there and back. There was a long walk on top of the train ride. Yet once there, she could always stay the night and see how Tooty was getting on. She wanted to remain a scullery maid, and most certainly wasn't going to be a lady's maid to Barbara. Yet there was one thing she was willing to do - make up and light her fire for her early on a cold morning. She would then sit in the armchair beside it and have a big warm up before she left to get on with the rest of her chores. As time went by they would chat while she was doing this, and some of the ice between them was breaking.

Then David hired a horse for Charlotte. He had just come back from Stockport and she had to be at the stable in Bowdon Vale for one o'clock.

At half past twelve she popped up to Gloria's room above the kitchen to get ready. She left the door slightly ajar, wanting to make as little noise as possible.

When she looked out, what a shock! Mr Carlton was standing in the hall. When had he got back? She had thought she was in the house alone. She stood there paralysed. She peeped round it again and again, but found it impossible to leave; he was packing something and making frequent journeys across the hall.

Now it was getting late. She should have set out for the stables some time ago. Once she did think she was going to get the chance and held the door slightly open, but just as she was about to dash out and down the stairs he appeared again.

Then, after a few minutes, she really did think he had gone. She crept out on to the landing, but yet again he came out. She had time only to dash across and hide at the bottom of the stairs going up to the next floor.

Now he was chasing the cat, and it ran upstairs past her. If he came up after it he would come face to face with her, and she would have to admit to everything. At one point he had only to look up and he would have seen her. She could see the grandfather clock ticking away the time, and she was horrified to see how late it was.

At her next chance she went back into the room and lay on the bed. It was hopeless. She had to forget all ideas of seeing Tooty that afternoon.

Then suddenly there came a loud bang from the backyard below. When she looked out it was only Mr Carlton again, sorting out some gardening tools and other things. 'He doesn't half take his time' she thought as she stood back from the window looking out at him. She glanced across at the other gardens, dreaming one day she might have something like them. She didn't feel at all afraid when he was facing her and she could see his face so clearly. She knew that with the lace curtain, even if he did look up, he wouldn't be able to see her.

She heard the clock strike one, half past one, then two. By now she had pulled a chair up by the window and was reading a book. Although she had always kept her eye on the time and knew it was late, she was still waiting for him to go away, for there were other things she wanted to get on with. It wasn't until the clock had struck half past two that he finally went.

She had wasted David's money on the horse and let them down at the stables, which meant she'd let David down too. He was known as such a reliable customer. She went to see him straight away, but his mind was on other things and he wasn't put out at all by what had happened. It seemed that the pressures of work were catching up on him, and he just wasn't interested. He also told her he was having trouble with Ethel, and wanted her to go.

'Let me know if you want any help with giving her a kick' Charlotte said.

That evening back at the house she told Gloria, 'That's the last time I ever go into the rest of the house. I got too confident. I could never relax again.'

She needn't have worried. There was too much to do, and too many other things to think about. One of the sons was getting married to a local girl, and there was going to be a big wedding at Bowdon Church, with lots of guests arriving and lots of cooking to do. Both Gloria and Charlotte were very, very busy.

The next day she suddenly heard a dreadful shouting from the stairs and hallway.

'Someone's drunk' said Gloria.

'What? Drunk before the wedding?' said Charlotte. She couldn't believe it, especially as the Carltons weren't the type to drink.

The noise got louder and louder. Now it sounded like a fight. Gloria went into the hall and Charlotte followed, forgetting her place. By the time they arrived the commotion was largely over. A woman came running down the stairs.

'They've taken him away, they've taken him away!'

'Who? Why? What do you mean?' asked Charlotte.

'The police, they've taken Mr Carlton, they say it's him that's been murdering all these women!'

It made Charlotte's blood run cold. Had she been alone in the house with the murderer? Two more women came downstairs, and Charlotte and Gloria followed them into the sitting room. They both sat down on an armchair in a complete state of shock as the other three women talked. As they listened, they discovered that Mr Carlton had been questioned about the murders at least once before.

'I wondered where he was when the first girl was murdered' said one. 'I knew he wasn't where he said he was.'

'He said other things I knew weren't true' said another. 'I thought it was because of his business. I did know there were things he didn't want to get out.'

'He's got two good sons' said the third. 'They tried to make up an alibi for him, said they'd been with him when they hadn't, but neither of them could stand up to it when they were cross-examined by the detectives.'

'I know. Then he tried to get away with it by saying he'd been on his own at the time.'

'He slipped up very badly with this latest girl, he'd have got away with all the rest of them otherwise.'

'He still might get away with some of it. It's only this latest murder they've arrested him for.'`

Both Gloria and Charlotte were surprised to hear there had been another murder recently. They hadn't heard anything about it. They were told 'Well I don't know how you've missed that, everybody's been talking about nothing else since it happened this Tuesday.'

For a minute or two they all just sat round in a glum silence. Then one of them said, 'It's that girl's mother who I really feel for. She had lunch with her daughter at half past twelve, then at two o'clock the police arrived to tell her her daughter had been found strangled at the back of Spring Bank.'

Charlotte rose from her chair. 'The girl was murdered between half past twelve and two o'clock yesterday!' she cried. She went rushing out of the room and racing straight up the road to the police station as fast as her legs could carry her. She rushed straight in. 'He didn't do it, he didn't do it!' she was panting. The murder had taken place just at the time when she had been watching Mr Carlton so closely while she was trying to sneak out to go to the stables.

When she came out of the police station she walked across the road into Bowdon Church, as she wanted to pray. Then she went back to the house. She walked in through the front door, which was wide open. Nothing mattered any more; so much was being brought out into the open.

129

She went straight up the stairs to Gloria's room. Mrs Carlton came out of the dining room and saw her go. Charlotte stopped to turn round and say to her, 'He didn't do it.'

Mrs Carlton walked slowly back into the sitting room, completely numb. Charlotte felt certain that everything would soon be all right.

She went to bed very early that night in Gloria's room, the one above the kitchen. She was completely worn out with it all and settled down for the night. Gloria slept in the room above.

Then at half past eleven she was woken up by Mrs Carlton knocking on the door. She stumbled out of bed to find Mrs Carlton standing on the landing outside.

'They've charged him with murder' she said.

'They can't!' she exclaimed almost shouting it, 'He didn't do it, I know he didn't!'

'Well, they've charged him.'

Charlotte felt sick. They hadn't accepted her alibi. 'Come downstairs and I'll make you a cup of tea,' she said to Mrs Carlton, and as they went down side by side, Charlotte had her arm round her, trying to console her. She sat her in the sitting room and went into the kitchen to make her a hot drink. Yet nothing she said would give her any assurances. Mrs Carlton had no faith in justice.

'I know a solicitor just across the way; his back garden almost joins on to yours, I'll see him about it' said Charlotte.

She too was beginning to lose her faith in justice. She remembered being told what her grandmother had said about the police when Robert Peel had first started the Metropolitan Police Force in 1829, that it wouldn't work.

She was not the only one saying they would never be able to overcome the problem of corruption. Yet as time went by people started saying there was more going for the idea than against it, and maybe it was a good idea. There were also fears that if the police were heavily criticised when they couldn't catch someone they might try too hard and get the wrong man. Now Charlotte feared it.

It was very late at night when she walked across the back garden and into the one next door. This way she would come to a low wall, easily get over it and into David's. She continued on her way, walking through weeds and long grass. It was a moonless night and she couldn't see very well as she struggled through it.

Then suddenly she stopped dead. Someone was standing in front of her; someone from a very long time ago. It was Rodney.

'Don't go, don't go!' he told her. She cried at the sight of him. Everything she had ever felt for him poured back again. Her heart was full of yearning and longing from all those years ago. Could this really be true?

He looked so calm, yet so concerned and wise, exactly as she had always remembered him. She knew he was right. She should not go.

She strolled slowly back to the house and lay on the bed. What had made her have such a vision? When this sort of thing happened it was supposed to be the subconscious mind working away. Whatever was it she was trying to tell herself? Did it really happen? Maybe Rodney really had come down from heaven to warn her about something.

She never knew how she managed to sleep so soundly that night, but she slept through until five in the morning. Then she saw Rodney again. He came to her in a dream to say 'He's done it.'

She sat upright in bed and said it back to herself loud and clear: 'He's done it.' She knew who he meant. David.

She could not go back to sleep. What was it David had kept saying to her - 'You will say you were with me when I was at piano practice?' Just what had he been up to?

She could not get up and have breakfast as though nothing had happened, not after that. How could the son so calmly put off the big wedding and have a small one instead with all this going on? At nine o'clock she went to do some shopping. She was going up to the grocer's. And then she met David at the gate.

'Charlotte, you will give me an alibi won't you' he said. 'You will say you were with me last Tuesday, that won't be difficult as I know you were on your own.'

She gave her usual answer, 'Of course I will,' but now she knew she was talking to the serial killer. She wondered if it would be her turn next.

Then he said, 'Charlotte, will you marry me?'

'No.'

'Charlotte, I may soon be dead, and if you are my widow you will be able to live in the house you wanted. I'll make sure I buy one.'

'But you won't be dead for a long time.'

He looked at her with haunted eyes. 'I'm going to hang.'

She did not try to argue with him. He knew that she knew the truth.

'Why did you do it?' she said.

'I hated those women, they were tarts.'

'Queenie wasn't a tart! It broke my heart when she died.'

'Queenie was a whore. The world has been cleansed of her sins now she has gone.'

'How could you dare show your face inside a church after all that?'

'The church says everyone is redeemable. I always felt safe there, my soul is safe The judge will say 'May God have mercy on your soul'.'

Then he told her he had killed another woman, and the body had never been found. He even told her where he had left her, in an alleyway leading from Green Walk into Park Road.

She screwed up her courage and went to have a look, but she couldn't see it. She didn't have the stomach to look too hard. The girl had been missing for some time.

She began to wonder if his confession made sense. Perhaps he hadn't done it after all; she certainly hoped not. She decided to challenge him about it.

'You'll have to forgive me for saying all that,' he told her. 'I was covering up for someone.' He wouldn't look at her.

'You said some mighty peculiar things.'

'I was in a complete dither about everything.'

'Who did do it?'

'I thought I knew, but I didn't.'

'Is Ethel mixed up in it?'

'I thought so, but I thought wrong.'

She didn't want to go into it any more. She was traumatized by it all. What was the truth about it all? But she didn't want to lose him. She still felt fond of him, and she couldn't help thinking of the money he had. One day he might be a big help to Tooty.

'Who is Ethel?' she asked him. 'There was always something fishy going on there.'

'Ethel may be a distant cousin of mine. Her parents lived in France. When the revolution became inevitable they went to join the poor and pretended to be poor themselves. They lived in a slum until they managed to escape to England. But they were always afraid to let it show that they had money. They carried on living in poor areas.'

Charlotte felt that this explained Ethel's rough and coarse voice, which was of a type she particularly detested.

David went on, 'She was the daughter of an old schoolfriend of my grandparents. When my father died, when I was very young, Ethel's mother was always very good to me, and my aunt always felt in debt to her.'

'Was there money involved?'

'Yes. An income might have been stopped if we'd refused to do anything for her.'

Charlotte married David six weeks later, in a church some way away. They didn't tell anyone about the wedding. It was tricky; she was a poor servant girl and he was a gentleman. They made plans for how they might in time be able to live more openly together.

At first they lived in West Road. He told his aunt everything and she accepted it. They could live there for a while as the two other servant girls had left. The assumption was made that Charlotte was a servant, but she would still frequently nip across the back garden to Gloria's and help out with the Carltons. David was in Stockport a lot, and Charlotte would then stay in the little house he had bought for her in Altrincham, one in a row. There were rows and rows of them, but not many of them were back to back. They were nothing like as bad as the slums in Stockport or the lanes off Chapel Walk, Regent Road as it became.

'It's all the money I could get hold of,' he told her. 'Any other income I have will all go when I die.'

'That won't be for a long time' she laughed, feeling embarrassed that he spoke of such things. She now felt certain it wasn't he who had killed the women.

Chapter Eight

THE LITTLE HOUSE IN CALAIS

But Charlotte's first suspicions had been correct. David was tried, found guilty and executed three months later outside Chester Castle. The body of the last girl had been found; there was evidence on it to show it was he who had killed her. They found it in the alleyway where he told Charlotte he had left it. She hadn't been able to find it herself because it was deep in the undergrowth and half hidden under a hedge, and she hadn't wanted to look too closely. There was also plenty of evidence that he had killed all the other girls.

For a short while after his death she thought she was pregnant, though it turned out to be a false alarm. As someone who had been widowed, being single wouldn't have mattered nearly so much. She wouldn't have been considered a fallen woman, but at the same time she didn't want it to get out who she had been married to. Fortunately, even though the papers were full of the murders and trial, they had married in secret and no one knew about it. Nor had she been seen out with him much, if at all. Yet it still worried her - if people did find out, would they hold it against her?

She suffered bereavement and wanted him back, but she wanted the man she had thought he was, not a murderer. She didn't want him back as a husband. It was Rodney she wanted.

She wondered what the point was of hanging someone. How could they find out what makes people kill if they kill them in turn, instead of studying them and doing research? How can they always be certain they've got the right man? Look at how they had arrested Mr Carlton.

'If only I could have David back as a close friend, a man that's been cured and is happily leading his life,' she'd say. She kept away from Bowdon. There might be someone there who knew. She remained in the little house that David bought for her in Altrincham. With a wink and a nod he had managed to leave her a little bit of an income; after all, he was never a scrupulous solicitor. He knew how to bend things.

The little house was in William Street, next to Tipping Street, and as time went by the clouds began to lift. The estate was known as Calais, and people said this was because such a lot of the Irish moving in there seemed to be called Callaghan. In fact it reminded some of Wales, where everyone seemed to be called Jones. The houses had been built a couple of decades ago, and were nothing like as bad as the ones off Chapel Walk (now Regent Road). For one thing they all had pavements and for another, they each had a kitchen sink. Some of these were still outside, but at least it meant no more sharing.

One day while strolling along, Charlotte passed a house where an Eileen O'Reilly, a youngish woman, about the same age as Charlotte, was outside cleaning the window. She was singing an Irish song:

'If you're Irish come into the parlour, there's a welcome for you here

If your name is Tom or Adrian or Pat, as long as you come from Ireland there's a welcome on the mat'

A Mr O'Callaghan was walking past and he laughed and said, 'That woman's asking for her kitchen to be very full.' Another Mr O'Callaghan walking in the opposite direction laughed too and said, 'In another hundred years time everyone will have some Irish in them.'

Charlotte looked amused. 'My name's Ann Smith' she told the woman. 'May I come in?'

'Of course!' said the woman, and she changed the words of her song: *'If you're English, come into the parlour…'*

She already knew the woman a little, although they had never been on much more than 'good morning' terms. They had a cup of tea together, both avoiding the subject of the famine in Ireland. Potatoes had been the main source of food for the workers, and in 1845 a vital crop of potatoes had been destroyed by blight. How they dreaded it. Some had noticed it coming, for they could see the black spots on them. In 1846 it struck again, thanks to non-stop rain.

Charlotte only vaguely knew something about the potato famine. She knew it was being said that the English had done virtually nothing to help. They just sent some maize to start off with. The whole of Ireland belonged to Britain in those days, yet the British government gave no protection to the peasant farmers. They were too poor to pay rent for their land, and a lot of them originated from Scotland because the same thing had happened there. The English had thrown them off their land. But when this happened in Ireland it was a lot worse, for many more starved.

Charlotte was willing to believe all this. She knew the English were a mixture of races and that many wicked people were about. She also knew that the Irish were basically the same, a mixture. How those who starved must have hated the ones that left them to die, and for no other reason than greed. Charlotte couldn't tell them not to hate. But she also knew that some people look for a reason for hate, and that hate begets hate. She feared that one day some of them who were in no way affected would be saying they hated the English for no good reason.

Eileen O'Reilly, who had lived through it all, showed no hatred. She kept mainly to the subject of how very kind her own landlord was in Altrincham.

'Very wise' said yet another Mr O'Callaghan, when he heard about it. 'Just stick to that when speaking to Miss Smith.'

But he knew that deep down Eileen O'Reilly was after the blood of the man who would have happily seen her starve. She dreamed of reform. She dreamed that one day he would be put on trial and she would be there to give evidence against him. She would then be able to say it all.

Gloria visited Charlotte. She was leaving her job and Mr and Mrs Carlton were asking where she was. Charlotte let the house in Calais, and moved back into the house in Bowdon. The boys were now both grown up and left, but Mr and Mrs Carlton wanted to keep the house should ever they come back with grandchildren. They were often away and said they needed someone to always be in the house.

When they were there Charlotte would only use the back door, and she would only go into the rest of the house to work or to go to her own room above the kitchen. She found it unbelievable that this was the same house she had once had to live in in so much secrecy, and now she could use it all, the wash-house, the cellars, and stairs to her room, whenever she liked. When they were away she would use the front door, the big one that she had once found so daunting. She'd been promoted as high as she wanted. She had the run of the house. She wouldn't want to own it; it would be too much responsibility.

Most of all it was the back garden she loved. She was free to go into it whenever she liked. She grew potatoes and vegetables for everyone.

One thing she was afraid to tell people, for fear it would encourage rude jokes; the reason one part of the garden was so fertile. This was where she had once used a hole for a privy. One day when she was alone in the house she brought in some flowers and was putting them in a vase in the sitting room when she looked up to see Barbara, of all people, coming up the drive. She looked nervous. It had obviously taken her some courage to come.

'Barbara, what can I do for you?' she asked as she opened the front door, and Barbara stood there still as well dressed as ever. But why was she here?

'Charlotte, I read about David in the papers' she said. 'I'm so sorry you've been widowed again.'

'How did you know he was married? How did you know I was his wife? You'd better come in.'

They went into the kitchen while Charlotte made some tea, and then went up to the sitting room with it.

'I met Tooty and we're friends now, or at least most certainly not enemies, but she let this slip out' said Barbara. 'I promise you, no one knows.'

They went into the kitchen while Charlotte made some tea, and then went up to the sitting room with it.

'You're very kind Barbara' said Charlotte. 'I was all right for a while with David and then I suffered delayed bereavement.'

'I think you might understand my situation' said Barbara. 'I am married to a brute of a man. When he was being horribly strict with our daughter I had to put my foot down. He was demanding that I should beat her, and then he would start to get violent with me. One day I had to lie across her on the floor to protect her and he threw me off. Then it got so bad that it was my daughter protecting me against him.'

'Where is she now?'

'She's with her nanny at home.' She began to cry.

'But Barbara you have money, can't you get away?'

'It's not as simple as that. Money helps, but it doesn't solve it. In fact money is what it is all about. He keeps wanting more of it.'

They went out for a walk together round Bowdon. 'People vary so much' said Charlotte. 'Some are nice and some are just dreadful.'

'I was a dreadful child.'

'Barbara, children are just awful, and you'll probably find at the end of the day you were no worse than any of the rest of us.'

They walked down towards the new railway station, Bowdon Peel Causeway. "Why don't they call it Hale Station, as it's in Hale? said Barbara.

"They probably will one day' said Charlotte. 'But for now, as there are only a few cottages scattered around it and as it's for people in Bowdon, they might as well call it Bowdon Peel Causeway.'

They then decided to go straight down to the other Bowdon station, on the corner of Lloyd Street and Railway Street. They weren't certain that the new station had been built yet and only Barbara thought it had. In fact Peel Causeway Bowdon Station was not built until 1862, and the name was changed to Hale Station in 1902.

Charlotte could really sympathize with Barbara's feelings over the death of her mother. Clearly they'd been very close. She knew how she had felt about her own mother.

When the train came into the station, Charlotte said to her 'You know I will always help you. Come and see me and Tooty any time.' But she never saw Barbara again.

* * * * * * * * * *

Charlotte found it difficult to stay in one place. It was as though she had a streak of gipsy in her. When there were no tenants in the house in Calais she would go back there to live, yet she would always go up to the house in Bowdon every day to work. She never stayed in Calais long; one reason was the overcrowding, which made her feel she shouldn't be there. Although many residents had their own privy at the back of their house like her, some of them didn't. In one case six households shared a single privy. She knew other people would sometimes come into her backyard and use hers. There was no piped water or underground drains for them. There was only one pump and one wash house for 80 houses. At least there was a large square for children to play in.

Sometimes they would have another girl staying in the house while she was there in Bowdon, but none of them would stay long. Right at the top of the house there was an attic with a very small window which let in hardly any light. It had a sloping roof so you couldn't stand upright easily, yet one girl, Maggie, had always wanted to be there. Did it make her feel safe?

Then she left very suddenly. She had heard about the murders. She asked Charlotte about them and, was horrified when she realised she was living so near to it all, never dreaming that Charlotte had been married to the murderer.

Maggie had a man friend of her own who had often been to the house. As they went he made a remark about the summerhouse in the front garden. 'I hope it can't talk' he said.

Charlotte told them she hoped it couldn't too. She remembered some of the times she had spent in there with David. It had been very easy to get inside without anyone seeing you, especially at night. It was just over the wall from the road and even nearer still to next door's front garden.

Mr and Mrs Carlton didn't mind these girls only coming for a short while. In fact it suited them. They only wanted Charlotte. They told her, 'You can always have a home here.' But at the same time so much pressure was being put on them. There was great overcrowding in Altrincham. Every year through the 1850s there was an outbreak of typhus and dysentery, and every year the health inspectors tried to prevent it. People in Bowdon were being criticized if they had a lot of space, and many of them continued to fear that there was going to be a revolution like the one in France.

Another girl who stayed had a vision of her mother, who had recently died of cholera. She said her face was full of forgiveness.

Charlotte felt great pity towards her, as it suggested she felt guilty about something. She was certain she hadn't done anything bad to her mother. It was just a typical case of bereavement. She also felt certain her mother would be most upset to hear that she thought she had been a bad daughter.

It made her think of how she had seen Rodney. She persuaded the girl to stay a bit longer, telling her she wasn't ready to go to London, a girl of only 14 and so very lost in the world. The girl spent a lot of time upstairs on her own, and she was left to it; time is the great healer. Then she got a living-in job just round the corner, looking after a child of five. She and the little boy became great pals. 'Drop in and see me sometime' she said to Charlotte as she was leaving.

When Charlotte was in Stockport she went to visit a young servant girl, Betty, who lived just by the market place in a house called Stairway House. Catherine Mumford had written to her and asked her to go. Betty enjoyed the jovial services with tambourines held by Catherine and William Booth. She did hope they would start up the new mission they planned, and call it the Salvation Army. Yet far more than that they had something else in common. Catherine, Charlotte and Betty all hated the killing of animals for food.

Betty was an only child and had been brought up on a farm. Her family had lived in a tied cottage. Her father had done maintenance, feeding the horses and chopping wood while his wife had worked in all weathers and did long hours in the fields. Betty had been a milkmaid. Charlotte hadn't known before why they had always been considered so beautiful, but it was because they'd never had smallpox, so they had escaped the awful scars.

'Someone told me we get cowpox, and that stops us getting it,' Betty said.

Some doctors were trying to find a way they could make certain everyone got cowpox, to protect them from smallpox. Betty had heard it called vaccination, but others were saying it wasn't realistic. She talked of how she would go from stall to stall to milk the cows and how one day the farmer's wife came in to talk to her. They didn't like one another and her mother had told her to avoid her as much as possible.

The farmer's wife was trying to get her to work in the field as well, but it wasn't physically possible – there was no time. Betty got up from her milking stool and went into the next stall, but the farmer's wife followed. She waited until the milk was flowing before questioning Betty again.

In her anger, Betty unintentionally jerked the cow's udder and the cow stamped her back leg, which made the milk spill on to the straw. When Betty turned round the farmer's wife had gone. She wondered how she'd dared to stand up to her like that, never dreaming that she would soon be out of a job. There was now modern machinery and farm labourers like her father wouldn't be needed.

They were evicted two weeks later and their possessions were dumped out in the lane in the pouring rain. They got soaked as they walked away. Their only choice was to go into the town and beg.

Betty's father died shortly after this, but she and her mother managed to get a job at Stairway House. They had animals there and Betty looked after them, but she didn't want to eat them; she could see it wasn't necessary. She said, 'They preserve the meat by putting far too much salt in it, and then take away the taste of the salt by adding herbs. Why not just eat the herbs now that the taste of meat has gone?'

It was a great hindrance that Betty couldn't read or write. In fact she barely knew what writing was. Someone had explained to her how a mark on a piece of paper can mean a sound and if you put these sounds together it would make a word. It looked formidable, and she had no wish to try it. She felt certain she would never be able to master it, and if she made any attempt it would just show up more than ever that she wasn't clever. She could hold a pen, however - some people hadn't even learned that.

Yet Charlotte had a much bigger concern for her. Whatever happened, Betty must not get cholera. It looked as if her job would shortly be coming to an end in any case, so she took her to the big house in Bowdon. There were no other girls in the house at that time. She was still able to frequently visit her mother.

Charlotte was determined they should get rid of cholera, which had caused such devastation in her life and that of Alice Wood. It looked as if Alice Wood would not last much longer, and her family were again wondering when they should tell her they had found her daughter Rosemary. It would be a lie, but it would mean she could die in peace.

Then, great news – no lying would be needed, because they had found Rosemary's body. The police knew it was her, even after so long, because of her teeth. There were other things too. They had been interrogating two criminals down at the police station, who had broken down and confessed to many things. They gave the police information only the body-snatchers could know.

It was great news for Alice's family that she could now die happy. But Alice didn't die; in fact she made a complete recovery. And she saw to it that Rosemary was now buried in a very safe place; hardly anyone knew where she was. She didn't have a gravestone, so no one would know that a body was underneath. The land was consecrated.

Rebecca stayed on at Alice's as a live-in servant/secretary. She wanted nothing else but to stay, and they wanted nothing else but to have her. As time went by and more came out, it became more evident that it had been due to her that they had found Rosemary, and the night she had walked in and caught the body-snatchers red-handed. But it was a long time before it became certain. That didn't happen until two men were convicted of something similar in Knutsford.

As regards the Christian Book Shop, tired of all the criticism, Mrs Berry moved it up to the Polygon in Bowdon, next to the Griffin. It was very much needed. Since Mr Ross had gone no one had taken his place and in any case, the house had become so dilapidated they had little choice but to pull it down. There had been no point in repairing it; it had been vandalized so much.

Mrs Berry also did a delivery service for people in Bowdon who ordered cakes and bread, and sometimes Rebecca or Charlotte would deliver them. She also did quite a bit more inside the shop than just sell things. She had an area where you could sit and have a cup of tea and a piece of cake or toast, and there was also a bookcase full of books.

As Barbara's mother had predicted, Prince Albert died of typhoid fever in the Blue Rooms at Windsor Castle, in 1861. And as Charlotte said it should be, they were doing something about people getting the disease, not just royalty but ordinary people. Eventually more houses were built in Altrincham in the interests of better sanitation, especially around Stamford Park.

The news in Stockport was most distressing, not just about the disease. There had been riots between the English and Irish outside St Peter's church. The English were afraid the Irish would take their jobs. The trouble was very near to Stairway House, which worried Betty as her mother was still working there.

They did more building in Bowdon, on the corner of Richmond Road and East Downs Road, so Richmond Road now went all the way down Langham Road. In one of these houses at the very bottom was a very kind lady, a Mrs Waller, who took in fallen women and their babies. She kept them in her warm and cosy cellar, a log fire always burning, a comfortable bed, a cot by the side of it and a big rug to cover the floors. She also had an old man living in a caravan in her garden. A lot of people didn't appreciate her kind nature.

She was a devout Roman Catholic, and Doreen Fitzsimons would sometimes visit her. She had now moved away from Holly Bank and had settled in service in a house in a road called Norman's Place, just off Chapel Walk (Regent Road). It was in the same road where Rebecca had lived and was very securely locked up. It wasn't far from the slum where she had lived before when she had first met Charlotte and David, but she was far enough away and had enough space around her to feel safe from cholera. There was a standpipe at the house. Doreen was quite content there, though she only got a small wage. She still remained friends with Charlotte.

Meanwhile a rota had been drawn up at Bowdon Church, so there would be someone there every night to guard it. But the police felt certain they had got to the root of the trouble - one doctor was behind it all. They didn't have enough evidence to charge him, but they had enough to give him a heavy verbal warning. 'We know very well it's you,' they said. They released the two criminals who had given them so much information as they didn't want to discourage them; they thought they might be able to help them to clear up other crimes, and they turned out to be right.

They interviewed the boys involved, who said they had played a joke on the doctor. One of them had got into a coffin and jumped out at him when he opened it. The police also gave firm assurances to the church that Bert had in no way been corrupt. There had been whispers that he had been accepting a bribe, but he had just been very gullible.

'Doesn't it show that some doctors are only in it out of curiosity?' said Alice. She realised that there would always be rogue doctors, though were far more good ones. She thought how dedicated they had been when trying to beat cholera.

Some of the new houses built as an extension going down from Richmond Road were behind a stone wall with a gateway and a wood

146

just inside, and these were called West Bank. Charlotte would often walk through the gate on her way to visit Mrs Waller. She would walk along the path with its loose pebbles, passing all the trees. It made her think that there couldn't be anything else but peace in the world, but the papers were saying there was going to be a revolution in Russia like the one in France.

She remembered what Mrs Everett had said about it. She hoped that if there was a revolution the British royal family would look after the Tsar and his family, and they did seem very close. But Charlotte knew that in all classes some of these families were dreadful.

She listened to the birds singing and decided not to think about such matters. Some things were going well, and at least they had extended Bowdon Church as intended, so that everyone could sit down. They had also built St Luke's in the Vale and intended to have an infants'school next door.

How different it was here to the noise of the factories and the mills. Sometimes she would go down the steps at the end, cross the road and visit Mrs Waller and the girls with their babies. Sometimes there would be one, sometimes two, living in her cosy cellars.

After Betty left and got married Mr and Mrs Carlton had no more girls to live in and there was only Charlotte there, although Tooty was always welcome. Betty had also done much of her courting in the Summer House. She had been able to see her lover there waiting for her from the attic window. She had married well enough to be moderately comfortable, and she and her husband lived in Charlotte's house in Calais for quite a while, paying her a steady rent. She never did learn to read and write.

Some new houses had been constructed on a new road going from Richmond Road down to Langham Road. Two of these, which were attached to one another, were knocked into one and opened up as a children's home called Ingledene, with the support of the Church.

They later trained nursery nurses there. It was next door to Mrs Waller's and practically opposite to Mr and Mrs Carlton's. Tooty got a job there as cook, and it couldn't have suited her better. She had always said she would never work for the rich and idle.

* * * * * * * * * *

There was a woman called Mrs Waller who lived on the corner of Richmond Road and Langham Road, in a house called Church Bank. It was later demolished, and there are now flats there, still called Church Bank. Mrs Waller had an old man living in a caravan in her garden, who later died.

A lot of people failed to grasp the charitable nature of Mrs Waller's work in housing the destitute and homeless, yet many of them would do so well if given a chance. During the 1950s she would take in unmarried mothers and their babies, and as she was a Roman Catholic many of them came from the church. They were often Irish Catholics. Mrs Waller accommodated them in her warm and cosy cellar, as described in the story.

Sometimes one of these girls would pop up to the house where we lived, bringing the baby with her, and help my mother with household chores. At one time we had workmen in the house too, and one of them began interfering with me. I was only five years old.

Eileen, a girl we knew from Mrs Waller's, came up to the house to give my mother support in challenging this man. I continued to assume all grown-ups knew how to deal with such matters. Some people will wonder why my father, who was an excellent father, didn't see to the workman. That's anyone's guess, but if he thought it was a job to be left to women then he wasn't far wrong. My mother and Eileen soon saw the man off, while my father reported it to the police

It seems unbelievable to me that those girls may have been the unmarried mothers who had been so ill-treated by the nuns in Ireland. I still see them as big and important.

Another girl would come to babysit and sometimes she would stay all night. One morning my mother was calling and calling her, but we couldn't find her. Eventually we found her under the bed in her room, soaking wet and naked. She had been having a wash when the window cleaner started coming up the ladder. We all thought it was very funny.

Another time, a woman called Bridget came rushing round in the most dreadful panic. I was startled, because I knew that if a grown up is alarmed it must be something bad. She said her child had swallowed a threepenny bit. . My mother let her telephone the doctor, who came to the phone to reassure her that that it would be all right, the coin would come out the other end.

The emergency was over, and she and my mother went into the kitchen to calm down with a cup of tea. Yet I wasn't happy. This was the first time I had doubted a grown up's faith, for she and my mother seemed so confident that the doctor would be right. 'How could a threepenny bit do that?' I asked. But of course that was just what happened.

Many years later those cellars had to be closed down, as they weren't up to housing standard. There was quite a hoo-ha about it and it was featured on television. People asked if it was right, when there was such a problem with the homeless. At that time Mrs Waller hadn't had unmarried mothers living there for some time, but she did have some trouble with the flat upstairs, when a drug dealer moved in. The neighbours were appalled. None of them realised that this was only the beginning of a very big drug problem in Britain, and many innocent people were going to get involved in some way.

One Saturday night the dealer and his friends had a party which went on into the small hours. It annoyed Mrs Waller very much, as she was a Catholic and had to get up early next morning to go to Mass. She looked out of the window to see a big fat man on the grass very roughly handling two of her tenants from upstairs. He seemed to be going in and getting them out one at a time, so she phoned up the police.

They told her they knew about the problem and had found drugs in her house. The name they gave it was a word she had never heard before, and she had no idea what he was talking about. It turned out that the fat bully was a detective from the drug squad. It later emerged that one of the men had been across to Holland to get some drugs and they had sold him the wrong stuff. He paid a lot of money and it wasn't even a drug, which was why he was making such a disturbance.

They thought drug addicts would make a beeline for her house because it was opposite a maternity unit called Southfields, a place where they might think there would be a supply.

Although I say the problem was new to us, I had learned as part of my nurse training always to break disposable syringes because drug addicts would go through hospital dustbins looking for them. Later I worked in a hotel which was nothing more than a residential nursing home, on the corner of Chesham Place and Stamford Road. It worried me sometimes, especially when I was working nights, that a drug addict might start breaking in for something. An addict will look anywhere for his 'fix'.

One doctor once told us that if an addict tells you he has lost a syringe down the toilet you shouldn't believe it, he'd have gone down after it if he had done that.

I remember the days of playing with the children at Mrs Waller's with such joy. I used to jump over the wall into the garden next door of Ingledene, where the children's home was. It was so full of swings that it was more like a children's playground. I would go inside sometimes and have some tea there, and my mother would have two of the children over to tea in her house every Wednesday afternoon. I would go to their Christmas parties. I don't know if I was considered a rich little girl, but there was always a present for me in Father Christmas' sack.

We would leap over the wall at the end of Mrs Waller's, into the alleyway which ran beside the church. We would run up it to the curate's house, play with the curate's daughter, then go to the school playground and play with the caretaker's little boy, for the caretaker now lived in the old headmaster's house inside the playground.

As people grow older they so often see the past lit up in sunshine. Maybe this is why I am saying that those were the days. Now, where Southfields, Ingledene, Church Bank and the school and schoolhouse once stood, there are just a lot of boring old flats.

Molly Doreen Fitzsimons lived in Bowdon from 1949 until 1993, and then went to live in Altrincham until 1998. After this she moved to Stockport, where she died in 1999. In 1948 she lost her eight-year-old elder daughter, and then in 1969 her husband Frank died. She was never properly counselled on either occasion. It was a terrible shame, when so often the problem is that no one cares, but this was far from the case here. It was simply that people didn't know.

She had a younger daughter who was four when her first daughter died, and they kept it a secret from her. That's what they did in those days. They did it again when an old aunt died. It made this child angry, and turned her into a bully. This is what can happen when a death is kept a secret from someone so young.

Her husband's death was a dreadful shock to everyone. His own mother had only died six months before at the age of 90, and it is thought there was some connection. He died of a growth in the bowel, and some believe that bereavement can make a dormant growth start to grow again.

I think many people imagine death doesn't matter so much when someone is old, but it can sometimes matter a great deal. I even once heard of a retired Roman Catholic priest who was in a bad way because his mother had died, and she was 102.

The grief of bereavement can sometimes bring up other bereavements long forgotten; even the death of a pet can do this. I sometimes wonder if the death of Frank's mother brought it all up again about his daughter and it was this that did it.

They say your chances of getting cancer can be cut by 40% if you don't *eat meat. Twelve years before Frank died, he had tried vegetarian food. He said 'It's not bad, this stuff'. It wouldn't have taken much of a push to make him become a full-time vegetarian, but there was no one there to give him that push.*

LADY JANE GREY

victim of a power struggle

Between going to Bowdon Church School and Broussa High I went to Bowdon Preparatory School for Girls. It had been founded by a Mr and Mrs Edmondson, who had come back from Africa because of the unrest there. I remember that when the school first started it was so small that Mr Edmondson was able to take all the pupils to a concert in his car - there were only four of them. It had grown quite a bit bigger by the time I went there.

The school was on the corner of South Road and Stamford Road, but it has recently moved into Altrincham, to where Culcheth Hall used to be.

When I was 13 I went to Broussa High School in Broomfield Lane, Hale, which was then a girls' school. Our teacher, Mrs Moss, taught us about such things as the French Revolution and Lady Jane Grey. She taught history with great compassion, as though she wished she could have been there at the time to put a stop to it all, and I later found out that she was a very kind person. This was some comfort to me as there are so many dreadful people around.

She seemed to be of the opinion that Marie Antoinette, the Queen of France, knew little of the plight of the people, or at least that she could do nothing about it. In my story I don't have the same patience. Yet Mrs Moss got the message across; if you keep people very poor they will revolt.

Look at what happened in England to poor Lady Jane Grey, because of the male thirst for power. Lady Jane Grey was Henry VII's great granddaughter, daughter of Lady Frances and the Marquess of Dorset. She became known as the Nine Days' Queen after her very short reign before she was executed so that Mary Tudor could claim the throne in 1553. Her aunt, Queen Mary, daughter of Henry VIII, was given the name 'Bloody Mary', a charming nickname for a woman to have. Lady Jane's mother, Lady Frances, seems to have taken no interest in her at all. I realise she might have been very frightened, but she doesn't appear to have tried to save her daughter. I don't know how much time she had spent with Jane, but I do know that when Jane was 10 years old she was sent to live in the household of Katherine Parr. She was exposed to a strongly Protestant academic environment and became an intelligent and pious woman.

In the mad rush for the throne, Lady Jane Grey's uncle made her Queen of England. He was in a very strong position to do so, and no doubt it was with the full support of her father. She didn't want to be queen - there is a record of her saying, 'Have I really got to be Queen?' But it's obvious they thought they owned her.

After this everything went horribly wrong. She was taken to the Tower of London, convicted of high treason and beheaded. It's a long time since I sat at my desk in that classroom, but I will never forget how amazed we were that a father could put his own 16-year-old daughter at such risk.

It does seem to me that she was completely brainwashed. Of course it can be quite surprising how any of us can be so very conditioned, so frequently it's not until there is a crisis that we really begin to question what our beliefs really are. Yet at the same time, if people go on at us long enough, we may be capable of believing anything. This includes bad things about ourselves. Am I right in thinking that Lady Jane Grey was trying to justify all that they were doing to her?

Of course this may be also because she was frightened and didn't dare suggest that the men around her could do anything wrong. She had been convicted of high treason. This meant she could be burned at the stake or beheaded 'as the Queen pleases' (the traditional English punishment for treason committed by women). Then the Imperial Ambassador reported to the Holy Roman Emperor that her life should be spared and her death sentence was suspended. Everything might have eventually turned out all right for her, but her father and uncle wrecked it by supporting a rebellion against Queen Mary and her plans. It was a thoroughly dangerous rebellion to support and in particular it was thoroughly dangerous for Jane. She was still in the Tower of London convicted of high treason. Her father did at one time give support to Mary Tudor by proclaiming her Queen, but this was only in an attempt to save himself. He had completely abandoned Jane. It didn't do him any good - he too had his head cut off.

It is very typical of the kind of men whose only interest is to get control. It's all power and nothing else. There is no feeling for the women. When I was at school learning about this, we were all just coming up to sixteen ourselves. We talked of how this showed how greatly men can differ. None of us could imagine our own fathers doing such a thing.

Since then I have met many a man in a complete state of euphoria on the day his baby girl is born and he most certainly will never try to make her Queen of England but these days as well, I feel certain that such organizations as Women's Aid would get on to Mrs Moss about it and what she was teaching to all of the girls. That is about how some men's only interest is to get control. They're trying to get the symptoms of it taught in schools.

Can we really know what was going on? But I do know that the women's centres do courses for confidence boosting, and once someone has been brainwashed, it can be very difficult to get them to accept it, that it was all a terrible nightmare and that they are a lot of good. Her last words before she went to the scaffold were: 'Good people, I am come hither to die, and by a law I am condemned to the same. The fact, indeed, against the Queen's highness was unlawful, and the consenting thereunto by me: but touching the procurement and desire thereof by me or on my behalf, I do wash my hands thereof in innocency, before God, and the face of you, good Christian people, this day.'

How can anyone know what was really going on inside Jane's mind when she had been so brainwashed, so very conditioned, and was so bewildered and frightened? She was only sixteen and knew so little.

MONICA MILLS' STORY

There was another teacher at my school called Monica Mills, who would sometimes go well off the subject of the lesson. For example, she told us about an old man she would frequently meet on Hale Station while on her way home from work. He would tell her about all the battles he had fought in. She might have looked old and frail, but she wasn't simple. He had picked the wrong person; she had taught history all her life and knew her dates. She knew which battle she was talking about. She said 'He must be jolly old if he remembers that!'

I think this going off the subject makes it less boring. It offers a bit of light relief to the teaching, and many of the things we discussed were in fact educational. We girls talked the whole time about boys, and sometimes she would join in. What a shame she didn't know about misogyny, because she had met it all right – she just hadn't recognised it.

As a girl she had gone to a boarding school, and the pupils would sometimes be invited out to tea with people in the village. This would have been in the early 1900s. There was a young lad who would sit next to her, and they had a secret - they were holding hands under the table. She always thought of him as someone nice. She also thought very fondly of her father. She never married, but she by no means hated men. In fact she said she had never hated anyone in all her life, and I am certain this was true.

One day she went very far from the subject by telling us a story about a girl called Amelia who had been sneaking out from that strict boarding school to meet a boy. When she wanted to finish the relationship, he gave her a dreadful time. Yet he didn't cause her as much trouble as he had hoped because the headmistress, instead of scolding her, was most sympathetic. In fact she went as far as to tell her about a similar experience she had had when very young. She spoke to Amelia as though they were teenagers together.

Amelia was very relieved that the headmistress behaved as if she didn't know she'd been going to meet this boy when she had only been given permission to go to the shops. It was many years later that Amelia realised she had of course known all along. The headmistress was well satisfied that Amelia had learned her lesson, and knew to make certain there would be no more of it.

The police had been involved, as the boy had been saying he was going to drown himself in the river that flowed alongside the school, or throw himself off the school roof. He was trying to manipulate her with threats to self-harm.

Amelia didn't like it when her mother was brought to the school. 'Oh, don't tell her!' she had cried out to the headmistress, but she was told there was no choice in the matter. Very gently, the headmistress explained the situation to her, and when her mother arrived she too spoke to Amelia only in gentle words. Both women were aware that in a case like this it can sometimes happen that a man ends up killing a woman. There is more misogyny around than people realise.

OBSESSION AND JEALOUSY

The Thomas Craig case

Back in the 1900s, at around the time Miss Mills was a girl at school, a man called Thomas Craig was serving time in prison in the North East when he received a letter from his girlfriend Annie's sister to say that Annie was going to marry someone else, and he must leave her alone. Winifred, the sister, wrote, 'She cannot answer any more of your letters.'

What a shame she told him this and did not realise how dangerous extreme jealousy can be. Craig had been madly possessive and jealous before this happened.

Annie first met Thomas Craig in 1903 while she was living with her mother and sister. Unfortunately she went on seeing him even after finding out what he was like – even when he was on bail for house-breaking and causing grievous bodily harm.

When he was jailed for seven years she said she would wait for him. They wrote to one another quite often to start off with, and then her letters started getting less and less frequent. When he received Winifred's letter he immediately wrote to Annie. In the first line he told her he loved her, then after that he said one thing after another to show that he didn't. He also made a threat to kill her; he said he would put her where her dead mother was.

When he came out in 1910 after serving five years, Craig started looking for Annie. He went round to her house, but only the sister was there. Still not knowing how dangerous it was to talk about other men, she told him that Annie was now married, but refused to tell him where she was. Craig began to cry. She tried to reason with him, saying that even if he did find her she would refuse to speak to him. Craig told Winifred that if he met the husband first, Annie would have no husband left.

Then he managed to find Annie's brother in law, Thomas Priestman, who in all innocence gave him enough information to enable to find her.

Craig went to get a gun, then he went straight round to the house of Annie's mother in law and told her he was Annie's cousin. She said, 'Just hang on a minute, I'll get my coat,' and then took him round to where Annie was living with her husband. Annie was there baking cakes when they arrived. She didn't look up and see him, as she was expecting someone else and thought it was him. The mother in law went upstairs, thinking that as they were relatives they might have something private to discuss.

Then Annie realised who he was. Her husband was in the room busy doing something else and when he realised it, he went over to him and tried to shake hands with him. Craig refused and asked Annie why she had married him?' She said, 'Because I love him more than I love you.'

He started firing. Some of the shots hit Annie, but more hit the husband. She staggered about trying to help him. Eventually Craig ran out into the street and away. By this time Annie was hardly able to stand. Her husband collapsed dying in a pool of blood. Annie was taken to hospital to have a bullet removed from her breast.

When police went round to the house they found bullets everywhere, and began a massive search for Craig.

At the inquest on Annie's husband, she was asked if she had told him about Craig's threats. She said she had and that he had said they should keep all doors locked, but they got careless about this arrangement. They didn't really think he would carry them out.

Two days later a farm labourer handed them a note that he had found signed by Craig. It said that by the time they got it he would be dead and his body would be in the woods. They looked for it but couldn't find it. Meanwhile there were two burglaries not far away, and food and alcohol had been taken. A much bigger search for him was started and they found him asleep in a haystack on a farm. They woke him up and handcuffed him - he was very drunk. They found a loaded gun on him, and in the haystack they discovered letters, photographs, money, alcohol and cigarettes.

They took him down to the police station and charged him with the murder of Annie's husband. He said, 'I didn't mean to kill him, it was Annie I meant to kill.'

Craig hated Annie. He had to be the one who had control of her. He couldn't manage his fear of women and his need for them together. This is something women find out about a misogynist. It isn't that underneath it all he loves her really - his only interest is to get control.

While awaiting trial, Craig caused so much trouble in prison that they had to keep him in solitary confinement. Four wardens had to guard him while he was in the dock at Durham Assizes. He pleaded not guilty. He said he had intended killing himself as well as Annie, but he hadn't as he wasn't certain she was dead.

Annie said she had intended to marry Craig but changed her mind. Craig's father said that his mother had not been in her right mind when Craig was born and that Craig had been led on a lot by Annie.

Craig was sentenced to death. Five thousand people signed a petition saying that the jury had recommended mercy, but he was still executed.

After his death questions were asked. Why had the prison allowed

Craig's threatening letter to leave the prison? Why wasn't Annie given protection after he came out? The Home Secretary, Winston Churchill, was asked to give an explanation. It turned out that the prison governor had told the chief of police in her area, but she had not told them when she moved out of their jurisdiction. Maybe the truth is that neither she nor her husband knew how dangerous he really was.

Even if they had both had full protection from the police, would it have worked with someone as determined as Craig? One thing is certain, if she had have married him she would have had a dog's life.

MANIPULATED BY A CONTROL FREAK

Alice Hewitt's story

Whether or not you think Alice Hewitt committed murder back in 1863 depends upon whose account you read. It's rather like listening in court to the prosecuting counsel and feeling certain the man in the dock is guilty, but then after the defending counsel has spoken you feel he is innocent.

Your view will also depend on how much you know about men who hate women. Some people say it is not hate but wanting control, but when a man gets very aggressive I think you can only call it hate.

Alice Hewitt was the last woman to be publicly hanged in Britain. She was a young woman from Stockport, and only 27 when she died.

She had a boyfriend called George Holt. Many people detested him, and while many think he put her up to the murder for which she was executed, others believe he did it himself. These days, I feel certain, an expert witness, a psychologist or a criminologist would be called to give evidence.

Alice lived in Great Edgerton Street, in a two-up, two-down slum which is now the site of a car park off Princes Road, the main shopping centre in Stockport. She was a widow and lived with her mother, Mary Bailey, a cripple who needed a great deal of attention. She had caused Alice serious money problems. She got so little from the parish that she was dependent largely on Alice and her boyfriend, who had moved into the house to live with them. There was also another couple living there.

Alice had worked in a cotton mill, but because of the civil war in America she was now out of work, and in fact some people were near to starvation.

Alice would call herself Mrs Holt, although she wasn't married to George. In February 1863 she found herself pregnant with his child. He had a job and they should have been able to get by, but she still had to pawn some of her clothes.

Why? Was it Holt who was spending the money, or Alice herself? Did he drink? Most certainly he could get violent at times, which is a symptom of misogyny and a man who wants control.

Alice had a cousin in St Mary's Gate, off Churchgate, and one day she went to see him. It is said that this is where she met someone who started giving her ideas about getting her mother's life insured. It sounded as though she could make quite a bit of money. Later this made some people think she was planning murder. She might have been thinking of nothing else but getting by. We worry about pensions and we take social security for granted, but in those days there was no reliable financial help of this kind.

When her mother was ill with a bad chest, which went on for weeks, Alice went to the Union Workhouse in Shaw Heath and arranged for a doctor from there to come and see her. He diagnosed her as having chronic bronchitis and gave her something for it, but it meant Alice should forget all ideas of being able to get her any insurance as her mother would never pass a medical.

But Alice carried out a little forgery. Did George Holt put her up to it? Did the whole idea originate from him in any case? Did she fall for it all, never dreaming he had more than murder on his mind but plans for setting her up? It may all sound very far-fetched, but men like him sometimes do the most extraordinary and evil things. One common trick is to say that there are burglars in the house, get her to dial 999 and then when the police arrive go to the front door and say, 'Oh I AM sorry, she's always doing things like that.' This will quickly turn the woman into a nervous wreck, and she will then be persuaded to ask her doctor for tranquillizers. It may become so serious that she becomes known to the authorities. This could cause big problems if for example he is trying to get custody of the children.

Is the truth that Alice Hewitt was a sweet girl, expecting a baby and looking after a very sick mother, with absolutely no support? At the same time was being brainwashed and bullied by a brute of a man. How could she think straight with all this going on? How easy it is to say 'If only I knew then what I know now', but even if we had, even if we could turn the clock back, how much would we be able to manage?

Alice contacted an old friend, Elizabeth Well, a woman much older than herself, and the two of them went together to visit Dr Higginbotham. They pretended to be mother and daughter. It was a success and they got the paperwork to show that her mother was insured.

Then her mother's condition became much worse. Alice had been to Henley Davenport's, a chemist on Heaton Lane, and bought some arsenic. She had to go with a witness to sign the book, and said it was to kill vermin and lice. Did George Holt spin her some yarn? Did he send her, saying he had seen mice or something like it in the house? Or maybe he told her the arsenic was needed for something else?

Then her mother became violently ill and started vomiting. A Dr Rayner who visited her couldn't understand it, which is not surprising as he knew nothing of the arsenic. It might also be understandable that Alice didn't see the connection, if murder was the last thing on her mind. The doctor asked Alice to call again for further medicine, but she never came. Instead she called another doctor from the Infirmary, a Mr Barker, who diagnosed gastro-enteritis and gave her something for it. Then Alice brought in a Catherine Ryan to sit with her mother at night, as her condition was greatly worsening.

According to Catherine Ryan, Alice threw away her mother's medicine, saying it was making her worse. It may well have seemed like that to Alice if she was so completely unaware of what was going on. She gave her mother some brandy and something called 'root'. There was brown sludge at the bottom of the cup, and though her mother had been reluctant to drink it, Alice had insisted. She would naturally do this if she didn't realise it was poison.

It was after this last drink that her mother died, after having had several fits, which witnesses say greatly distressed Alice. Yet she did say that if her mother hadn't been dead by the end of the week George Holt would have kicked them both out. It sounds as if he was taking over the place.

In some ways you would think her mother's death was a relief, yet people who were there at the time said Alice was devastated.

It was several weeks after she'd been buried, and long after Alice had collected the insurance money, that a neighbour reported that the person who had passed as Mary Bailey in order to be insured was not Mary Bailey at all. That made the police investigate, and they searched the house. A cup was found with the remains of the arsenic, so the body was exhumed and an autopsy carried out. The conclusion was Mary Bailey had been murdered. Alice was charged and found guilty of it, and sentenced to death. She collapsed in the dock on hearing it. The jury had strongly recommended mercy, but she didn't get it.

Did George Holt do it? He had made a joke as soon as he heard that his mother-in-law was insured. He said, 'Go and buy charcoal to put under the old woman's bed so that she wakes up no more.'

Alice had in fact once accused him of trying to poison her mother. That was when she noticed that there was arsenic was in her mother's beer. But how serious was she being? Did she have any idea how right she was, that it was in fact arsenic, or was she merely being frivolous?

I've known of witnesses giving highly distorted evidence. In fact,

Alice might not have even have used the word 'arsenic' - it may have been an assumption made after the murder had been discovered. People do that sometimes. They hear or remember what they expect to.

George Holt gave evidence against her in court. He showed no compassion, and that's a symptom of men who want control. He had no interest in the three-month-old baby boy. The crowd hated him and jeered at him, and had to be held back to stop them attacking him. He escaped through the back door. He didn't visit her in prison or make any attempt to help her out with money. In court, he said he didn't even know the fiddle had taken place.

Alice's cousin, a clergyman, the Reverend Kilner, wrote to the Home Secretary asking for clemency, but this was refused and the execution went ahead.

On December 28th 1863 outside Chester Castle, unable to walk, Alice had to be carried or pushed to the gallows in front of a heartless crowd. She fainted when she saw it. Charles Dickens once wrote about such executions in the Guardian. Maybe it would remind some of those who go to football matches just to have a punch-up. An execution would be more than a pantomime, but a place to drink and start a fight. In this case the crowd had waited all night to see it.

Alice wasn't killed immediately; it took the hangman three goes to get the trap door to work. This terrible event caused a terrible outcry, and consequently all public hangings for women were stopped. The papers asked how we could call ourselves a civilized society.

If a woman was pregnant, she could still be sentenced to death, but she would have to wait until after the baby was born because they would not kill that too.

She did not want her child ever to know that his mother had been hanged for murder, and she repeatedly insisted that he must never did find out. He did not, but her great-great grandson did. He started making enquiries when he saw on her death certificate that she had died in a prison.

WILLIAM WOOD OF BOWDON

the 'Chimney-Boys' Friend'

William Wood was known as 'The Chimney-Boys' Friend'. I did wonder if I should bring him into the story of Charlotte. It seems unbelievable that during the 1800s they had the problems they did in Bowdon with the abuse of sweeps' boys. Legislation was not adhered to, one excuse being 'it's difficult telling on a neighbour'.

Sometimes Wood would bring in a private prosecution at his own expense, but he did much more than that, and not just locally. For example, he had large placards stating the law about boys in chimneys put up in railway stations all over the country. He wrote to Queen Victoria about a chimney being swept by a boy at Windsor Castle, and would challenge anyone, even a magistrate, if he thought it was going on in their household. He was a great supporter of Lord Shaftesbury, who also campaigned about it. Wood got very involved when the matter was discussed in the House of Lords.

Wood was a tough man, but a kind one. He was born in Bolton in 1782, the son of a Methodist. He became a woollen merchant and lived on Newton Street in Manchester, off Piccadilly.

In 1826 William Wood witnessed a horrific accident. A boy was climbing a chimney which joined another at the top, and fell down the ladder, where there was a fire burning. He died from his injuries. This event was the start of Wood's campaign.

He came to Bowdon in 1847, having retired, and moved into Willow Cottage in Stamford Road, where he lived there with his wife, two unmarried daughters and a son. There was also a servant living in the house. Wood had two more daughters. The two living there were schoolteachers and both became members of Bowdon Congregational Church, which their father joined a year later.

By the late 1850s Wood had moved across the road to another rented house, then called Oakfield Cottage. He was then Deacon of Bowdon Downs Church. He lived there with the same two daughters, his wife and the same servant, as well as Frank Redpath, a grandson, from Montreal.

Then age started to catch up on him. In 1862 he ceased to be Deacon. His wife died, and so did a daughter, Mary Hannah Brailsford, at the age of 51, who had married a Methodist minister.

Wood died in 1868 in his own home in Bowdon. His coffin was carried to Bowdon Church by six master sweeps from another town. The family have two tombstones and a headstone in Bowdon Churchyard. The servant is buried with them.

OLLERBARROW
FARM

This farm was a small one of about 35 acres, lying between Ashley Road, Ollerbarrow Road and Broomfield Lane. The earliest mention of Ollerbarrow Hall Estate was in 1406, when it was recorded as Owlerbarrow or Oulerbarrow, or Ellerborough, for 'oler' or 'aler', an alder tree, and possibly 'alder grove' implying a wet area, probably along the lines of Ashley Road.

Today the name survives in Ollerbarrow Road, with its Victorian houses. Ollerbarrow House, built about 1740 by the Ashleys, is the last surviving building from the estate. It is in the centre of Hale on the corner of Ashley Road and Leigh road, Leigh Road being named after the last farmer who owned Ollerbarrow Farm. It is constructed from small, hard made bricks from a brickyard at Riddings Road.

THE ORIGINS OF ALTRINCHAM

The town of Altrincham gets its name from a man called Tring, a Saxon settler. The place where he settled and raised his family became known as the 'home town of Tring'. Ing is a common Anglo-Saxon patronymic and can be found in the names of scores of English villages as a simple suffix, such as Buckinghamshire. Some of these places don't have a suffix, for example Hastings. Others have 'ham' or 'ton' added to them and are applied to mark the filial colonies sent out from this parental settlement.

The prefix 'alt' is a Roman word which means a hill, and the suffix 'ham' means the enclosure or home of a family. There's little doubt that this is where Altrincham got its name from – meaning the hill of Tring's enclosure.

Presumably the name was once spelled with a g. The 'ch' spelling is thought to have come about because parish clerks couldn't spell (spelling was more a matter of choice in days gone by), or because they couldn't read someone else's writing and mistook a g for a c. The old pronunciation with the g sound remained, however.

It was around the eighth century AD when Tring first lit his camp fire in what is now the Old Market Place, where the public house the Orange Tree and the old town hall, the Market Tavern, now stand. Tring brought with him horses, cattle, sheep and pigs and built a stout stockade to protect them against the wolves and wild bears which then roamed the forests around him. He then built up a farm consisting of huts for himself and his herdsmen, stables for his horses, byres for his cattle, barns for his crops of hay and corn and a place to stock wool after shearing. He found a plentiful supply of water from a spring in the higher land behind him known today as High Bank. A village grew up around his settlement.

As years went by the family colony and a branch of the family made themselves a home on a hill called Bowdon (the name means 'curved hill'), where they built a church of timber, Bowdon Church. A path to the church was cut in a direct line from Tring's enclosure through the woods we now know as Market Street, Norman's Place, the Narrows and the Firs, so Bowdon and Altrincham became closely connected.

As regards the history of Stockport, I know very little. However it is true that Martin Gilpin was the first vicar, and a very young vicar, of St Thomas' Church when it was first built for the growing populationof Stockport. He went to the Isle of Man after suffering ill health and died there aged 37. Living nearby on the Isle of Man were a surgeon called Gilpin and a girl of 15 called Mary Gilpin, but it is not known if they were related. Henry Bellairs became the minister afterwards and he did have a son who married an Elizabeth Isherwood. He left to be a school inspector.

There was a workhouse in Shaw Health, Stockport, which was later converted into a hospital called St Thomas', where I worked as a nurse. It is now closed down.

There were riots between the Irish and English outside St Peter's Church, which was quite near Stairway House.

BEREAVEMENT

'*Silence can communicate more than words. When my father died we would pass one another on the stairs and not say a word to one another. We would sit round a table and never say a thing. Silence can be soothing.*'

Wendy Bray, Diana Priest, Insight into Bereavement, 2006, **Waverley Abbey**

I read *Insight into Bereavement* after writing *A Bowdon Romance*. I did consider going over it a second time to see if I should put in any insertions from it, but decided not to. I think it better just to recommend it. Anyone with a Christian view of bereavement may find it helpful.

> *Give sorrow words*
> *The grief that does not speak*
> *Whispers the o'er fraught heart*
> *And bids it break*

William Shakespeare, Macbeth

Shakespeare was right. People want to talk about their grief, they want someone to share their pain with and when they do, they feel warmth.

* * * * *